A Wren Called Smith

Also by Alexander Fullerton
in Mayflower Books

THE WAITING GAME
CHIEF EXECUTIVE
THE PUBLISHER
STORE

A Wren Called Smith

Alexander Fullerton

Mayflower

Granada Publishing Limited
Published in 1974 by Mayflower Books Ltd
Frogmore, St Albans, Herts AL2 2NF

First published in Great Britain by
Peter Davies Ltd 1957
Copyright © Alexander Fullerton 1957
Made and printed in Great Britain by
Richard Clay (The Chaucer Press) Ltd
Bungay, Suffolk
Set in Linotype Plantin

To Ted and Mabel

I

Derby met me at the station, and when I say that he hadn't changed at all I mean that I'd allowed for him to be a few years older and I found him looking exactly as I'd expected. He was broadened, there was a touch of grey on each temple, his eyes were deeper. The old tweed jacket that he was wearing had leather patches on elbows and cuffs, and even that looked right, too, like the reefer he'd worn before we left Scotland for the Far East – oh, fifteen years ago! There'd been leather on that, too.

When he came up to me on the platform and shook my hand, I noticed one other difference – he smelt of cows instead of shale oil. Whatever Derby worked with, he smelt of, if it had a smell. He was a man who got close to his work. Submarines smell of shale, and dairy farms smell of cows – Derby had switched over. Now he shook my hand, beaming: suddenly he sniffed.

'Mike, you reek of shale. They still using that stuff?'

'Probably always will. I was just thinking, though, that you have a smell of cattle.' Frankly, I was rather disturbed to hear that I had the shale stink now. I was wearing a suit that had never been inside a submarine: it was new, as near as dammit, I'd only worn it a couple of times, and it had cost me most of a month's pay. That oil, I thought, must be in my skin. I wondered how long it had taken Derby, who had once been my Commanding Officer, to wash it out of his.

'Give me your bag.'

'Nonsense!'

'All right.' We headed for the gate. There'd been very few people on the train, and now when we'd finished greeting each other the short platform was deserted. Only a tall, bald porter was shifting crates of chickens about, close to a wall marked

Gents. We passed out through a gap in the fence, and Derby said:

'Couldn't live without her, now.' I glanced at him in some surprise. We'd all known, all those years ago, that he'd been wildly in love with his wife: we'd known it mainly because he'd written to her often and regularly and because wherever we'd been he'd never taken any interest in other women. He used to stay aboard, and write letters. But he wasn't the sort of man to make a display of his emotions, and this statement seemed out of character, somehow embarrassing. To cover it, I asked him how the boy was. The boy was the real purpose of my visit – a christening, and myself the Godfather. Derby ignored my question. He told me, his face glowing with pride:

'Use her for any damn thing you can think of.' Following his glance, I realized that he was talking about the Land-Rover. It was parked there ahead of us, in the station yard, and it was covered deeply in mud. I recognized it immediately as the vehicle I had frequently seen advertised in *Punch*. Only in those advertisements it was usually being driven over a cliff by a man in shorts and a pith helmet, and the caption referred to safaris or groundnuts.

Derby opened the rear door, and as I shoved my case in, a big yellow dog sprang from the front seat like a young lion in a circus. It only stopped itself by jamming its front paws against my chest. I dropped the case, and cracked my head on the top part of the door-frame: the dog began to lick my face. Its tongue was about a foot long, and black, and its breath stank of fish. I managed to drag the door shut between us, and by that time Derby was in the driving seat. He opened the other door.

'Jump in.' The dog was licking the back of his neck, but he seemed not to notice this as he started the car and crashed it into gear. A moment later, we were off. The Land-Rover had no acceleration, not in the usual meaning of the term: it simply set off at thirty miles an hour. The dog vanished abruptly into the cavern between the front and back seats, and I banged my forehead painfully against the windscreen. Derby muttered:

'Time they did something about these pot-holes.' We

steamed away at sixty, through a sea of flying mud. As far as I could tell, we were heading East. I asked him:

'Is it far?'

'What?'

I thought he hadn't heard me. I yelled, more loudly:

'Is it *far*?' He turned, and bellowed:

'Is *what* far, dammit?' The dog barked, suddenly, very close to my ear. Derby swept his left arm back, and knocked the brute to the floor again.

'*Your farm!*' But he didn't answer, only dragged the wheel over: we skidded into a sharp turn, hurtled sideways through an open gateway and down a sharp incline that was all mud. Dead ahead on our course was a barn or outbuilding, but somehow Derby missed it and we swung around its end into a littered yard at the back of the farmhouse. With something like horror I saw another yellow dog, rather bigger than this one but otherwise its double, staring at us from a doorway. Derby said:

'Place doesn't look much, this time of year. You ought to see it in summer.'

I had never met his wife before, but I did remember a photograph that he'd had on top of the steel cupboard in his cabin in the depot ship, and even now, all of fifteen years after it could possibly have been taken, I recognized her by my recollection of that pale face in its eight-by-six leather frame. She had the most wonderful eyes, a sort of slaty blue, and their colour in contrast with her dark hair was most striking. Irish, I thought. I told them that I remembered the photograph, and Derby seemed pleased. He was pouring whisky into three glasses.

'That went down with everything else. But I've got a copy. Show it to you, later. Soda or water?'

'Water, please. It should have been in colour.' She smiled, and at once I could understand how it had been that Derby, in our war-time travels, hadn't bothered with other women. No man in his senses would have! I asked her how she liked being

7

a farmer's wife, how it compared to marriage with a sailor, and she laughed.

'It's only the smell that's different.' Strange, that – it had been the first change I'd noticed, myself. And in another thing I'd been right, too: that soft voice was unmistakably Irish. We had our drinks now, and I raised mine.

'Here's to my Godson. What are we naming him?' Derby coughed, and his wife smiled. She murmured:

'We're calling him Michael.' I looked at Derby, and he said quickly, passing it off:

'Had to call him *something*.' As he said it, I saw that look of embarrassment in his face, and the sight of it took me back a dozen years and to the other side of the world: to a time when I'd been Derby's First Lieutenant in a submarine in the Far East. More precisely, to an evening which we spent drinking together in the wardroom of our depot ship, in Subic Bay in the Philippines. All that evening I knew that Derby had something he wanted to discuss, or tell me, and I waited patiently through drink after drink until the bar shut and he still hadn't brought himself round to the subject, whatever it was. But we'd served together for a long time, I knew him as well as he knew me, and there was no doubt about it, he had something on his mind. We went outside and leant on the broad oak rail, looking down at the trot of four submarines alongside. It was very quiet and peaceful and we could hear the water lapping down there on the saddle-tanks of the boats. Suddenly Derby said it.

'They're flying me home, Mike.' The statement came so abruptly and seemed so unlikely that I doubted if I'd heard it at all. If I had, surely he was pulling my leg.

'What did you say?' In public I used to call him sir, of course. But not otherwise. I asked him: 'What was that about home?'

'You heard me. Perhaps I should've told you before, but it wasn't certain. Now it is. It's – er – medical.'

'*Medical?* Oh, look, this can't —'

'Apparently I have T.B. "In a Mild Form", they assure me every ten minutes. Mild or not, I'm being flown home in a

8

couple of weeks. Don't commiserate, please.' That was an order – so I asked a question instead. The obvious question.

'Who'll take over?' Derby didn't answer, for a moment. He offered me a cigarette.

'Smoke?'

'Thanks.' I hated the idea of any new C.O. To me, that ship wasn't just a ship: she had a definite personality, and hers was the collective personality of our team. Without Derby, she'd feel like something new, foreign and untried. This wasn't good. I said:

'This is bloody awful.' I lit the cigarettes, and he puffed his into a hard orange glow that I could see in the corner of my eye as we leant there, staring down at our ship. Lying there in the still, oily water, she looked as relaxed and peaceful as her surroundings: ridiculously peaceful, considering that she was more a weapon than a ship. Derby told me:

'You'll be getting a new First Lieutenant.'

'A new —?'

'A new First Lieutenant. *You'll* be taking over the command, Mike.'

'*Me?*' It was unheard of! I hadn't even done a C.O.'s Course, I — '*Me?*' I turned to look at Derby, hardly believing that this could be anything but a joke. I saw at once that he was serious. He had that awkward look on his face: it must have been on his own very strong recommendation that I was getting the ship, he'd paid me the compliment and now it embarrassed him that I might feel grateful and try to express it. He said quickly, pushing himself back off the rail:

'See you in the morning, Mike. Come to my cabin, after Hands Fall In. We've a lot of ground to cover.'

I watched him walk slowly in through the screen door – all the C.O.s had their cabins on this deck. It struck me suddenly and forcefully that in a few weeks I, too, would be quartered here! I, with my own Command! It was a wonderful thought, but I let it ride in my imagination for a minute and then it was less wonderful than frightening. Oh, in seniority and submarine experience I was just about due for it, anyway – but normally a First Lieutenant would finish the ship's commission and then go home for a Course. I've always loathed courses. After that as a new C.O. he'd spend some time in a training flotilla, running a non-operational boat as a practice target for destroyers and frigates. But now suddenly this promotion bridged at least a year, and while as a First Lieutenant I'd had everything at my finger-tips and felt no false modesty about my competence or efficiency, the idea of a Command made me feel green, nervous and unsure. It was such a vast step in responsibility, and my problems now would be so entirely different. Still in the same ship, I'd be seeing and thinking with different eyes and a different mind: what could be even more difficult, the men who'd been used to me as Number One might find it hard to reframe me as their Captain.

I couldn't help the doubts creeping into my mind. Whether it was really a very wise decision. Whether I was up to it. How it would affect the efficiency of the boat.

These thoughts had been racing through my mind as I climbed down the broad steel ladders into my own cabin flat. The cabin was in a hell of a state – I'd changed in a hurry. Now in more of a daze than a hurry I went about the process of undressing and turning in. I'd started off astonished, then passed to a stage of some elation: now I was simply scared. I kept thinking that in only two or three weeks' time I'd be taking *Slayer* on her seventh Far Eastern patrol, and this time every decision would be mine instead of Derby's. The more I thought about it, the more terrifying the idea became. I lay naked on my bunk with a sheet over me to intercept the direct draft from the nozzles on the ventilation trunk, and with the familiar hum of the fans in my ears I sweated myself into a half-sleep. There was an unreality about all this, now, I'd wake in the morning surely, with nothing of it left except a thick head. I thought: I'm half awake but half asleep too, all of this is a dream, the result of too many pink gins. After three weeks on patrol without even a smell of alcohol, the stuff went to a man's head – gave him nightmares. In the morning I'd tell Derby about it and he'd laugh. Well, *certainly* it was ridiculous! – he was as fit a man as I was, they'd cart me off on a stretcher before they invalided Bill Derby!

10

The humming of that ventilation trunk crept into my half-conscious mind and it sounded like the boat's motors, full ahead and grouped up for top speed and I was standing groggily with my back against the Control Room ladder and I was watching the depth-gauge and the angles of the hydroplanes in their electric repeaters. I felt half dead, I'd had only about ten minutes sleep, and heavy sleep at that, since I'd come off watch, and now we were at Diving Stations with a target in sight and I was wishing I'd stayed awake. There was a taste in my mouth that might easily have come out of the engine-room bilges, and I had difficulty keeping my eyes open. But Derby was at the periscope and he'd just passed the order to blow up all six tubes, and that meant a target worth sinking, worth eighteen thousand pounds' worth of torpedoes. I stood there facing the trimming telegraph, and we were heavy in the bow, so I had the ballast pump sucking on the forward trimming tank: but we were still heavy, and the Second Cox'n was holding his fore 'plane at hard-a-rise to keep the boat at her depth. Even at that, we were at thirty-two feet instead of thirty, and behind me Derby muttered:

'Keep her up, Number One. For God's sake, keep her up.' The trouble had started when he'd had to order this burst of speed, full ahead group up, when the boat still had a bow-down angle: it'd been something of a miracle that we'd held her anywhere near periscope depth. But the pumping was beginning to tell, now, the Cox'n was gradually easing his wheel and we were settling with the bubble in the middle of the spirit level. I reported:

'Thirty feet, sir.' I switched the lights over to tell the stoker below to stop pumping, and to tell them for'ard to shut off the tank.

'Stand by all tubes.' Derby spoke quietly, and it was only because it was dead quiet in the Control Room, all of us waiting for his orders, that anybody heard him: the closer Derby got to a target, the quieter he became. But then, he never made much noise, at any time. He'd have been no use at all on a parade ground, or in a battleship. Here, he was at home.

All you could hear was the ticking of the log, and the hum

11

of the motors driving the submarine under twenty degrees of wheel on to an attacking course. We were holding our depth all right, now, so I glanced quickly round to see what was going on. The men at their stations had their eyes on Derby's, they watched, as I did, the flickering light that his eyes took from the periscope lenses, hard light from the bright Pacific up there over our heads: it flickered from the bubbles dancing around the upper lens cutting through the blue water, it shone in the twin mirrors of his eyes so that they burned like a cat's in the half-dark.

'Slow together.' The telegraphs whirled over, silently because the bells were disconnected. An acknowledgement, a report.

'Both telegraphs slow ahead together, sir.' And Ellis, the Mechanician, reported back a message from the Tube Space:

'All tubes ready, sir.' Ellis was tall and thin: his Adam's apple wobbled when he spoke and he was much more at home adjusting and repairing his instruments than he was in using them. Now he stood in his usual uncomfortable-looking stoop in front of the row of firing levers, with a telephone set clamped over his balding head, and to him that 'All tubes ready' from up for'ard meant that the Torpedo Gunner's Mate had withdrawn the pins from the firing mechanisms on the tubes so that when he, Ellis, pulled these levers in the Control Room, the torpedoes would be ejected from their tubes. What happened to them after that would be the Captain's business, the Torpedo Officer's, the T.G.M.'s. Ellis's interest in the matter ended with the functions of the apparatus for which he was personally responsible.

Derby leaned back from the periscope, and pushed up the handles. Dawson, the Outside E.R.A., dropped the lever to send the long brass tube hissing down into its well. He did it with his right hand and at the same time he used his left to wipe sweat out of his eyes. It left a smear of grease across his forehead and the sweat still ran. Just for'ard of the Control Room, the Navigator called from the chart table.

'Enemy speed sixteen, sir.' It was only a suggestion, really, the closest estimation he could get from the plotting diagram. But Derby accepted it.

'Set sixteen.'

'Set sixteen, sir.' Haines, the Torpedo Officer, made the adjustment on his Attack Machine. It was a box-like affair, full of dials and arrows and figures in little windows. Derby told Ellis:

'Tell the T.I. the target's a destroyer.' He gestured briefly with his finger-tips, the Dawson brought the periscope rushing up into his hands. Haines muttered:

'D.A. twelve, sir.' Derby had his eyes jammed against the lenses. He said:

'Bearing – *that!* Range – *that!*' The man standing behind him read the bearing off the calibrations on the deck-head, where the periscope fitted into its gland and the silver drops of sea water glistened down over the grease. The Navigator bent quickly over his plot: the point of his pencil broke, he swore and snatched another out of the rack. He had a dozen of them there, carefully sharpened. Derby spoke quietly and evenly, as if everybody did this every day and nothing could possibly go wrong. 'I'm – I'm seventy, on his starboard bow.' He stepped back, and Dawson dropped the lever again: but only a dip, at once Derby raised his hands, and the periscope thumped to a stop and shot up again. Derby was being careful: at this close range, there was a risk of the periscope being spotted by the enemy. If that happened, the situation would be drastically changed, and the submarine would be at the receiving end instead of attacking. Destroyers were not the safest targets. The Navigator reported:

'Enemy speed sixteen point five, sir.' Derby bent to the periscope.

'Set sixteen point five. D.A.?' The Torpedo Officer twiddled the speed knob and peered at his dials.

'D.A. still twelve, sir.' There was a pause while we waited, and everybody was tense with excitement except Derby, and he, as usual, looked relaxed and cool. I had always envied him that quality, that astonishing self-possession at moments when nine men out of ten would be sweating blood. He was looking into the periscope in the manner of a scientist staring quietly into a microscope. His voice wasn't sharp or hurried when he spoke.

'Stand by.' Ellis's throat wobbled like a turkey's and he echoed:

'Stand by, sir!' He had his long fingers curled round the firing lever for Number One tube, and the whole length of that arm of his was shaking with excitement.

It was precisely at this moment that my dream became a nightmare. It was *I* that had passed the order: 'Stand by!' It was the periscope I was facing, its wide handles in my hands, and when in sudden horror I straightened and looked around me at the scene in the Control Room I saw a stranger's back where I should have been, behind the 'planesmen: I looked around, and saw that every man had his eyes on mine. I couldn't face them, couldn't stand to have them see the panic in my face: I thrust my eyes at the bifocal of the periscope, and I'd hardly glimpsed the destroyer when she *turned towards. She'd seen us and she'd turned to ram and I was in Derby's place at the periscope and I opened my mouth to order us deep and I couldn't get the words out, I couldn't speak. I was frozen at the periscope watching the Jap destroyer coming for us with her bow high under increased speed and the bow-waves curving out high and white and infinitely menacing. I struggled to tear myself back from the periscope, but I couldn't move: I strained to shout an order, but my jaws were locked.*

I woke suddenly, drenched in sweat, and as I broke out of the nighmare I heard my own voice shouting:

'Sixty feet!' Then, awake, as I lay gasping for breath and listening to the pounding of my heart, a sleepy voice called from some near-by cabin.

'Shut up, you silly bastard!' I couldn't have disagreed with him, whoever he was – it was the way I felt, too, about myself, and the nightmare. But it had seemed so real, so detailed, and – up to the point when it had changed into nonsense – an exact reproduction of an attack we'd made on our last patrol. The ending had been entirely different – Derby had fired six torpedoes and hit with one, blown the destroyer in half and sunk her within a mile of Jap troops on the coast. Near Bin Dinh. In the South China Sea, just a week ago.

I didn't sleep again that night, and I didn't tell anyone about the dream, either, next day. But a fortnight later when I took over the ship from Derby, it was still in my mind, and in a way I dreaded this stepping into his shoes. Luckily, we were rushed: there was so much to do, so many practical things to think about, that my worries and imaginings faded into the background. . . . But that is an entirely different story. I must get back to this one where I left it – after the war, and I was spending a week-end with the Derbys on their Sussex farm.

It was later in the evening, on the day I'd arrived, and Derby's wife was upstairs with the baby: she'd been up there a long time, and we were consoling ourselves with the end of the whisky and a warm glow of reminiscence. I murmured:

'That was quite a party, your farewell.'

Derby nodded. He sat there staring into the fire and nodding in a happy, thoughtful sort of way. He hardly ever smiled with his mouth – you had to know him well enough to look at his eyes, if you wanted to see any expression of his feelings or his mood. He said, slowly, watching the flames:

'Poor old Withers had a dreadful head, the morning after.'

'Poor old Withers' was Lieutenant-Commander C. J. Witheringham, Royal Navy, the Executive Officer of our depot ship in Subic Bay. He was a General Service man, not a submariner, and he was one of the stupidest people I have ever met. In the flotilla, he was a standing joke. You'd only have to mention his nickname, 'Old Withers', and before you'd said another word everyone'd be grinning, waiting for another story with a funny ending. Well, Derby'd been told that he was being flown home, but at the last moment the authorities changed their minds and decided that he'd go by sea instead, in a fast Norwegian freighter that was sailing direct without convoy: and Withers was going in her, too. He was overdue for home leave, as he'd been in some remote shore base in

15

Australia for several years before he'd come to this depot ship: apparently Their Lordships had forgotten his existence. You could hardly blame them for that. Anyway, we gave a farewell party for the two of them, and it turned out to be a riot.

That afternoon, Derby and I and a few others had been swimming from Pequena, a small island out in the middle of the bay. There was very little to do, in Subic, except swim and drink. Once or twice a week we'd be invited ashore to the American mess, for supper or a cinema show – sometimes they had real live entertainers, even film stars. These were provided by an organization known as U.S.O. – rather like our own Ensa, only more glossy. But that was about all we had, by way of relaxation. We got along very well with the Yanks – we liked their films, and they liked our gin. They weren't allowed liquor in their own ships and bases, poor fellows, and any evening at the time our own bar opened in the depot ship, you could stand on the quarter-deck and see boats approaching from every point of the compass.

Well, by the time we'd shifted into evening rig and hurried to the bar, the party was well under way. Several of the Yank submariners had arrived, and of course there were officers from all our own submarines in harbour. Withers was there, and when we arrived they were pulling his leg about how he would spend his first night in England. Withers was blushing furiously and assuring them all that he never did anything of the sort, it wasn't worth the candle. He used phrases like that. It was really astonishing that anyone as completely stupid as Withers had managed to remain a bachelor for so many years.

The gin bottle went round, and Derby signed the chit. It was custom for a man joining the party to do that: a sort of entrance fee. The lucky ones, or the canny, were those who arrived early, when the round was small. I sent the bottle on a second lap, and signed a duplicate chit, and that finished the bottle. In one corner, five or six chaps had started a game of Poker Dice. We all drank to Derby and Withers, and an American started to make a speech, but he was shouted down.

Some time or other, we had supper. Then, back in the bar,

16

there was singing. The Americans listened attentively while a bunch of our people sang 'Cats on the Roof-tops', a song that deals exclusively with the nocturnal habits of cats. An American shook his head slowly as he remarked:

'You goddam British. All day you're so damn polite a guy'd think you got born in plastic packs, but come evenin' you're all hollerin' in tune 'bout fornication. *Gets* me.'

'Don't *you* sing?'

'Oh sure. But not —'

'Well, *sing*, then.'

The American called to some of his friends:

'They wanna hear us sing, fellers.' The suggestion was taken up immediately. Our guests huddled together in a corner, placed their arms round each other's shoulders, fixed misty stares on the deck-head, and gave tongue. The first two lines of the song, so far as I remember it, were –

'When the Angel of the Lord
With his tu'rble swift sword—'

I forget what it was that the Angel of the Lord did with his terrible swift sword, but the last line I remember very clearly because it was repeated after each verse and much more fervently than the rest.

'WHEN THE ROLL IS CALLED UP YONDER I'LL BE THERE!'

Derby whispered to me:

'Mike, this is rather embarrassing.' I agreed. I had never heard anything quite like it, certainly not in the wardroom of one of His Majesty's ships. The Americans were standing at attention, now, bawling the chorus. Derby said suddenly:

'Let's go ashore. It's the only way to stop them.'

So, presently, we straggled to the quarter-deck and piled into the launch, which happened to be alongside and was just going inshore for liberty-men. On the jetty we were joined by Haines, *Slayer*'s Torpedo Officer: he had little Mary Lou with him, and he didn't much want to join us, but the Americans insisted, because they wanted Mary Lou. She was a

17

Wren, the only one in the Philippines, and she worked with two American girls on CTF 71's Cypher Staff. She and her two friends were always surrounded by Yanks, and consequently we hardly ever saw her. As Withers would have summed up, it wasn't worth the candle. Mary Lou was small, dark and very good-looking. It puzzled me that young Haines should have got her to himself for an evening: it also explained his absence from the party, an absence which had seemed to me to be plain bad manners when the occasion was a farewell to his own C.O. Now I understood, and I didn't blame the lad a bit. In fact, I was rather proud of him. After all, there were about forty thousand men in the Philippines, not counting Jap snipers in the woods, and there were only three women.

Mary Lou told us brightly:

'This is my farewell party!' An American corrected her.

'You got it wrong, Baby. This is Lootenant-Commander Derby's farewell party.' From somewhere behind us, Wither's voice floated out of the dark:

'And mine!' The American coughed, and added:

'Oh, sure! Commander Witheringham's, too.' We'd all forgotten Withers. Derby called over his shoulder:

'You all right, Withers, old man?' We were struggling inland up a steep, red-earthed track that led to an out-of-bounds liquor shop. Withers didn't answer, he was puffing and panting and one of the Americans was helping him along as if he was a dead-beat prisoner on some death march. Mary Lou, shrill with excitement, asked Derby:

'Are you going on the *Gangerolf*, too?'

'The what?'

'The Norwegian ship. I'm leaving on it tomorrow and —' Withers had shouted something. It sounded like his last gasp. Derby asked, solicitously:

'What's that, Withers?'

'I said, *Security*. Careless talk costs lives.' It was the sort of thing that only Withers would have said. He'd have done splendidly in A.R.P. Derby told Mary Lou:

'The answer is Yes.'

18

'Oh *goody*!' She detached herself from Haines and an American challenger, and, rushing across the track, seized Derby's arm and hugged it. 'What *fun* we'll have!' She danced along beside him, and really you'd have thought that he'd always been the only man in her life.

The liquor shop loomed up ahead. It was set back off the dirt road, and although it was a filthy, dilapidated shack in daytime, now in the dark with the palms behind it and the moon behind the palms, and yellow lamplight filtering out of the doorway, it looked almost beautiful. Withers panted:

'I don't know that we ought – ought to – I mean, isn't this one of those out-of-bounds places?' We assured him that it was quite all right, and an American voice commented:

'Wha' d'*you* care, Commander? You'll be the hell an' gone, this time tomorrer.' We filed into the dimly-lit shack, and the proprietor, a little fat Philippino wearing foul shorts and a torn vest, came up smiling and bowing as if he was the head waiter in a West End grill. His smile was wide, oily and avaricious. Derby ushered Withers to the fore.

'What you like, gentlemans? You care for gin, brandy, pompom?' Derby pointed to Withers. He told the proprietor:

'This is the senior officer. Ask him.'

'Oh yes, Captain! For you brandy, pompom?' Withers hesitated. An American urged him on.

'Come now, Commander! Let's have a snap decision.' Withers looked thoroughly frightened. He asked the Philippino:

'What is – er – pompom?' The man beamed, rubbing his fat hands together. The Americans were all grinning: they'd been here before.

'Please, Captain, I show! This way, Captain, splendid pompom, all for you!' He was indicating the curtained entrance to some sort of back room, and it was clear that Withers was expected to pass through. He stepped nervously forward, and Derby and I moved with him, but the Philippino held up his hands in horror.

'Please, gentlemans, one at a time!' He took Withers by the

arm, and half dragged him through the doorway. Only a second later, we heard a shrill yell of alarm, and Withers reappeared, travelling backwards at speed. I caught him, otherwise he'd have sent Mary Lou flying. The Americans were howling with laughter. The proprietor appeared in the doorway, an annoyed look on his face.

'You don't like, Captain? Cleanest girl in Subic, officers-only girl. You don't believe me, Captain?'

Withers was as white as a sheet. He told Derby, in a trembling voice:

'There's a woman in there. A *black* woman.' He whispered, so Mary Lou wouldn't hear: 'She's *naked*!' An American, choking with laughter, told him:

'That's pompom, boy!' Mary Lou had heard, all right. She shrieked with excitement.

'Oh, let me look!' Derby grabbed her, held her back as she started forward. She fought him. '*Please* let me look!' Withers said, sternly:

'*Certainly not.*'

'Oh, don't be so —'

'As senior officer present, I forbid it.' An American spoke up in a tone of disgust.

'Pull'n his goddam rank!'

Derby saved the situation by ordering brandy all round. A cheer went up, and while the proprietor bustled round pouring what he called brandy out of a petrol can into mugs made out of cigarette tins, we pushed Derby and Withers up on to the counter and sang 'For They are Jolly Good Fellows.'

Oh yes, it was quite a party, Derby's farewell. The whole flotilla had hangovers, next day, and two Americans went into hospital, poisoned.

But the rest of this yarn is Derby's. He told it to me while we sat late over the fire, in his Sussex farmhouse, twelve years later. His wife joined us – the baby'd gone to sleep, at last – and she curled up on the sofa with her head on his shoulder, and he rambled on, staring into the fire. Occasionally I'd ask a

20

question, and sometimes she'd remind him of some point he'd forgotten: now and then, I'd throw another log on the fire. The rest of the time, Derby just talked: and here it is, the story of his passage home.

II

Gangerolf had been a fruit ship, before the war. That is to say, she'd been completed at the war's start and had barely finished her trials when her speed had been put to its first practical use in evading seizure by the Germans. She was a slim, trim freighter of five and a half thousand tons gross, according to her pre-war register, and her owners had intended her to carry fruit from Australia and South Africa to balance the diet of over-eating Scandinavians. Now her refrigeration machinery had been removed, and the holds which it had been intended to cool were used for war equipment instead of oranges and grapes.

Captain 'Happy' Christiansen had driven her at her trials, and now, still in command three years later, he recognized no other home. He was a huge man with a red face and a pock-marked nose, and he had acquired the nickname 'Happy' because he was one of the most morose and belligerent Masters who had ever sailed the oceans. He was known for two other qualities: his almost unbelievable capacity for whisky, and his superb seamanship. 'Happy' drank a bottle of whisky every night, and he had never been seen drunk, ashore or afloat: he handled his ship with a smooth artistry that brought murmurs of admiration from any watching seaman. He was intensely proud of being Norwegian, and he nursed a deep hatred for Germans and a bitter contempt for Swedes. He tolerated Englishmen, and loved the Scots.

Derby knew nothing about any of this, when the depot ship's motor-boat with its engines churning noisily astern brought him face-to-face with the Jacob's ladder that hung from the *Gangerolf*'s starboard quarter. He'd recognized the ship as soon as he'd spotted her, because he'd looked her up in the Recognition Manual, and her silhouette with the sharp bow and streamlined bridge and cowled, slanted funnel, wasn't easy to mistake for any other. He'd noticed, as the boat closed in, that she was extremely well kept, clean and tidy. In fact, he had a first impression that this was a ship run by seamen. The boat shuddered to a stop abreast the dangling rope ladder with its wooden rungs, and Derby put a hand under Wither's elbow to steady the older man as he grabbed awkwardly at the air. Derby was feeling out of sorts, his head ached and he hadn't smoked a cigarette all day, but Withers looked like a corpse. Withers looked really sick. Derby's head was just about splitting, and really it wasn't his fault: he'd had no intention of drinking any of that Philippino brandy, but he'd been compelled to, by the Americans. Standing on top of the counter under their close and suspicious observation, not even a member of the Magic Circle would have been able to get rid of the liquor except by drinking it. Normally he'd have poured it on the floor, or out of the window. But Withers – that was a different matter. The old fool had suddenly entered into the party spirit, he'd decided that these Yanks were jolly good fellows too and it would only be civil to drink with them as they apparently expected. He'd swallowed a lot of the poison, and now he was sick. Derby just about pushed him on to the ladder, and shoved him up it until, several rungs higher, a burly Norwegian leant down and took over the weight. Withers scrambled aboard, ill and dishevelled. As soon as he was out of sight, over the side, Derby waited until the boat rose to the top of a swell, then stepped on to the ladder and clambered up. The Norwegian was throwing a rope's end down to the boat, for the baggage. He said to Derby, over his shoulder:

'Velcome aboart *Gangerolf*, Mister.' Derby thanked him.

'Where's the Captain?' The big man had dragged up a suitcase, and now stood staring at it as if he thought it was too small and ought to be thrown back.

'Captain?'

'Uh. Where do I find him?'

'No, Mister. Not afternoon. Captain sleep.' He dropped the rope back into the boat, and waited while a second suitcase was attached. He said:

23

'Sailing seven, eight o'clock. *Everybody* sleep now.' Withers sidled up between Derby and the seaman and asked, in a voice that was little more than a whisper:

'Where's my cabin?' The Norwegian swung a third case over the rail, dumped it beside the others, and turned to answer the question. But first he looked at Withers: his inspection was like that of an anthropologist having his first close-up of some unusual species of monkey. His interested stare drifted up over Wither's spare and slightly stooped frame, and rested on the pale, anguished face. Then he looked away, quickly.

'In von moments, I showing you.' He flung the rope's end down to the boat, and Derby heard him mutter: 'Gutt Gott a'mighty! Oh my! Oh Lort!' The boat was shoving off, and this was the last case now, safely aboard. The Norwegian threw one last, almost fearful glance at Withers. Then he bent, stowed one case under his left arm and took another in each hand. He set off for'ard, and Derby, struggling with the last two cases, followed: Withers, empty-handed, brought up the rear. They filed in through a painted steel door, and along a thwartships passage to the foot of a flight of stairs. Here the Norwegian jerked one shoulder at a green notice-board, and Derby, following the direction, found a cabin-plan pinned to it. His name and that of Lieutenant-Commander Witheringham were bracketed together against the figure '3'. He pointed at it, and told their guide:

'Cabin three. Both of us.' He moved out of line, to peer into an open doorway on the opposite side to the stairs. It was the dining saloon, panelled in some dark wood. The gloom of it was enlivened by a pair of silver nudes, rampant, on each panel. One long table ran down the centre of the saloon. The Norwegian jerked his head angrily, indicating the stairs.

'Op!' Derby shook his head.

'You lead. Show the way.' The man nodded.

'Follow, pliss.'

There was a landing at the top of the stairs, a space the size of a small room. It was furnished with a sofa, a round table, and a brass thing which at first looked like a spittoon, but was most likely an ash-tray when there were passengers aboard. In the for'ard bulkhead were double doors, and Derby struck one of them with a suitcase so that it swung open. This was evidently the lounge: it ran the width of the ship, and was furnished with armchairs, sofas and tables. There was a radiogram in one corner. The Norwegian looked impatient. He told Derby:

'This firs'-closs lounge. Com.' Derby asked him:

'How many classes are there?'

'Von closs, all firs'. Follow, pliss.'

From the landing, a narrow passage led aft on each side of the ship. Right at the start of the passage on the starboard side was a door marked '3'. The big man dropped one case, and used that hand to fling the door open.

'Pliss.' Derby turned, politely.

'After you, Withers.' Withers stepped into the cabin, and Derby followed him. The Norwegian lumbered in behind them, and the three of them, plus luggage, were all that the cabin could hold. For a moment, it was standing-room only. Then the Norwegian grunted, and backed out. He shut the door, and they heard his heavy steps on the stairs as they turned to survey their new quarters.

There were two bunks, one above the other. Withers said, pointing at the lower of them:

'If it's all the same to you, Derby, I'll take this one.'

'Suits me.' Derby stepped up with his toes on the edge of the lower bunk, and thumped the top one with his fist, to test the mattress. It didn't give, much. He climbed down again, jammed his cap on a hook on the inside of the door, and sat down on one of the suitcases to take off his shoes. Withers was still standing there with his cap on, staring at the furnishings of the cabin. Derby told him:

'I think I'll get my head down, for a bit. Why don't *you*? Sleep's by far the best remedy for hangovers.' Withers shook his head.

'I think I'll unpack, first.' He coughed, and said stiffly: 'Get things squared off and ship-shape.' Derby had removed his shirt, and was climbing into the top bunk. He said:

'Suit yourself. But don't make more noise than you can

25

help, squaring things off.' He thought: The little horror's feeling like death, but even *in extremis* he's jumping at the chance of getting his stuff out first and pinching three-quarters of the stowage space. Well, let him. He lay back, and closed his eyes. This was *good*. Out of great relief, he murmured:

'Good-night.' There was a moment's silence, then Withers asked:

'What did you say?'

'I said, *Good-night*.'

'But it's only four o'clock!'

Oh *my* God! Derby thought, I've got this all to myself for four or five weeks! He turned on his side, and peered at Withers over the side of the bunk.

'*Good-afternoon*, then!' Withers stared back, blankly. He still had his cap on his head and he looked as if he was wondering where to be sick first.

It was a thump that woke Derby, the thump of some heavy craft coming alongside rather clumsily. He looked at his watch – five-twenty. Remembering Withers, he peered down into the cabin through half-open eyes: there was no sign of the man, but plenty that he'd been at work. Two of the cases were empty, their lids thrown back, and the third, also open, held a mountain of rubbish, mostly screwed-up newspaper. Withers had certainly 'squared things off' before he'd turned in. He was turned in, all right – fully dressed, even the epaulettes still in the shoulders of his shirt as he lay, breathing heavily, with his face close against the bulkhead. Derby slipped quietly down from his bunk, and opened one of his own cases to find a towel and shaving kit. He crept out, in search of a bathroom.

Half-an-hour later, feeling surprisingly well, he was dressed in Red Sea rig and had the rest of his gear stowed away in the few spaces which Withers had left unoccupied. While he'd been bathing and dressing there'd been a great deal of noise on deck, shouting and orders and feet stamping about. He'd thought: Either we're sailing earlier than expected, or Mary Lou's arrived on board and they've cleared Lower Deck to see

26

her come. He knew nothing of any other passengers – this ship was controlled by the American sea transport people, and apart from his own orders to join her for passage, he was ignorant of her destination, route or cargo. None of that mattered, anyway: all he needed to know was that he was headed for England. He'd been married only a few weeks before he left, and it seemed about ten years ago instead of two and a bit.

He'd closed his suitcases and was sliding them carefully and quietly under the lower bunk, when there was another bump. It was louder than the first, and the ship quivered under its impact. On the upper deck, a voice rose in passion.

'*Clomsy basstud!* Vy you not stay home in the goddammed States, take bloddy lessons?' The voice faded into a torrent of angry Norwegian muttering. Other Norwegian voices joined in obvious sympathy. Withers, who had seemed dead, sat up with a jerk, like a Jack-in-a-Box, and struck his head on the bottom boards of the top bunk. He struggled to get his feet out of the sheet in which they were entangled.

'What was that? Derby! What's the —'

'It's all right. Nothing to worry about. Some boat bumped alongside and scraped the paintwork. Why not go back to sleep?' Withers lay back on the pillows, and Derby noticed that he looked worse than he had before. The sheets, of some coarse material and by no means new, were less white than his face. He groaned.

'Derby. I feel awful. *Terrible.* Couldn't you —' Derby closed the door quietly behind him, and found his way out on to the starboard side of the passenger deck. He walked aft, to the break where a ladder led downwards, and leaning there on the rail he had an uninterrupted view of the activity below.

Alongside, on the starboard quarter, an American landing craft rose and fell to the gentle motion of the sea: at the top of each lift, Derby could hear the bump and scrape of her against the ship's side. It occurred to him that if the Norwegians had put their ladder on the other quarter, the leeward side, they'd be losing less paint now. He saw that the landing craft was full of scruffy, sullen-looking young men: they wore all sorts of clothes, but predominantly what seemed to be some sort of naval garb. One by one, not in any kind of hurry, they were climbing the Jacob's ladder on to *Gangerolf*'s deck, and there, still bearing that dull, obstinate look as of men uncaring but somehow moving against their will, they were falling into two lines. Here and there, American army men lounged with automatic rifles cradled loosely in their arms: several of them were chewing gum, and all of them looked terribly bored. Among them stood a man whom Derby at once classified as the ship's Chief Officer: he wore khaki, with three blue stripes on each shoulder, and a cap with some unusual insignia over its peak. As each man reached the deck and turned to join the long, listless line, the Chief Officer stared at him with an expression of cold, if not venomous, dislike. The prisoners looked exactly like Germans, but Derby couldn't see how that could be, here in the Philippines. His doubts were to be answered immediately.

'*Gottdam bloddy Hons!*'

Derby turned, and saw a very large man with a red face and a pock-marked nose standing just behind his left shoulder. He must have approached very quietly: glancing down, Derby noticed that the man's enormous, hairy feet were bare. He wore khaki shorts and an unbuttoned bush-shirt without any badges of rank. He was chewing a black cheroot, and he kept it in the side of his mouth as he told Derby, bitterly:

'I asking th' bloddy Yank Admiral, I asking him: Bloddy Hons in th' *Gangerolf*? Yars, he say, You take 'em, boy. I tell him: *Drown th' basstuds*, I say, I don' want 'em! Ve got enoff back home, in Norvay! Drown 'em like cats, I say.' The big man shrugged. 'Make no bloddy difference, I got 'em.' He grinned suddenly. 'I reckon that's how it is, vith Admirals, huh?' He took the cheroot out of his mouth, and spat some of it over the side. 'You passenger?'

'Yes. My name's Derby.'

'Christiansen. I am Captain of this ship. Velcom, sir.' They shook hands. Derby asked him:

'Tell me, Captain. Where'd these Germans spring from?'

'Bloddy submarine. Yanks sink 'm. Big von, brings ball

28

bearings to th' Japs. Bloddy Svedes making plenty ball bearings these day, selling 'm to Germany.' Derby nodded. He knew about that. He said:

'We get some too, though.' Christiansen raised his bushy eyebrows.

'So? Is bloddy nice of Svedes, huh, to sell to both sides? Make plenty for both, make tvice moch money. You know vot is Svedes, Commander?'

'Uh?'

'*Basstuds.*' He nodded, spat out some more of the cheroot, and drove the point home. '*Basstuds.*' Derby leant back on the rail. Most of the Germans were inboard, now, and one party of them had been split off from the rest and herded for'ard, where they and their guards had disappeared under the overhang of this deck. He said, diplomatically:

'You know more about them than I do, Captain.'

'*Know* them? *I* say I know them! In my cabin I have photo, I show you. Photo, King of Sveden giving bars of chocolate to bloddy Hon soldiers, on Svedish railway platform. Is Hon propoganda photo, I show you! You know vot them basstuds doing in that train, Commander?'

'No. What?'

'On vay to attacking *my* country. Shoot my vife, maybe, murder my boys. Vot the Svedes doing eh? Give 'em ball bearings an' chocolates! Sure, Germans, ve don' aim stop you: you go t'rough, murder Christiansen's boys! Fine, yust so long you buy plenty ball bearings!' The Captain chewed furiously on what remained of his cheroot. Then he chuckled

'You know somethin', Commander?'

'Well?'

'Reckon them steel balls is only kind Svedes has! Right?' Derby laughed.

'You could be right, Captain.'

'Could be? Gottdam *sure* I'm right.' Derby asked him:

'Where are you putting those Germans?'

'Nomber t'ree hold. Fitted special for troops. And t'ree cabins, too, for bloody officers.'

'*Three* cabins? How many officers are there?'

'T'ree. Orders say, keep 'm separate. So I put 'm in cabins down below, move Chief Officer and Engineer and Steward to passenger deck. Chief Officer okay, but my bloddy Engineer gone mad! I telling you, Commander, Engineers is all awkward basstuds. Make trobbles, alvays trobbles, out of boggerall make bloddy shindy. In your sheeps, you have Engineers make trobbles?'

'Well, no, Captain. I had a darned good one, in my last ship. Believe it or not, he even used to stand a watch on the bridge, when we were on passage. Not on patrol, of course. But he's a damn good chap.' Derby was feeling homesick, already.

'Vot sort sheep, yours?'

'Submarine. "S" class.'

'So ... And you – Captain?' Derby nodded.

'That's right.' Christiansen stared at him, nodding slowly.

'So. Commander, you drink visky?'

'Certainly.'

'Good. Good.' Christiansen threw the mangled stump of his cheroot over the side. He grasped Derby's arm. 'Com. Ve go my cabin, drink visky.'

Christiansen's quarters were large, considering the size of the ship, and well furnished too. He had a day-room, a sleeping cabin and a bathroom, and these took up two-thirds of the deck space at that level. The other third was occupied by the chart-room, and from it an internal ladder gave access to the bridge. Christiansen showed Derby round, and they spent some time playing with the Radar set, which had only recently been installed. Then Derby saw, with some surprise, that a large part of the chart-room was filled by what looked exactly like a carpenter's bench. He pointed at it.

'What – er?' Christiansen beamed. It was obvious that this was the *pièce de résistance*, and that in drawing attention to it he had done the right thing.

'This my vork table.' The big man opened chests and lockers to display saws, hammers and other tools. Fitted boxes held nails and screws, bradawls and gimlets. Planes and chisels – and every other woodworking implement in every shape and size. He told Derby:

'Here I am enjoying harbour time. Qviet time at sea also, fine vay for passing time.' He looked at Derby, and nodded. 'I like.'

'What do you make, Captain?'

'*I show you?*'

'Please do. I'd be most interested —'

'So!' Christiansen's grin was almost wider than his face. He opened a locker on the other side of the chart-room; really, it should have held sextants, star globes, distance finders. Derby saw that it was full of toys. Christiansen lifted one out, very carefully, and set it down on the bench. It was a farm cart, drawn by a wooden horse on wheels, and so well made that it could have been real, looked at through the wrong end of a telescope.

'That's wonderful, Captain. And all those —'

The Norwegian, chuckling quietly to himself, brought them all out and set them down for inspection. There were ships, areoplanes and Noah's Arks. Dolls' Houses, windmills: many other things.

'This —' He indicated the assembled toys with a proud sweep of his enormous hand. 'This I make the last two month. Not so bad, huh?' Derby asked him:

'What're they for, Captain? I mean, what d'you do with them?'

Christiansen didn't answer. He stood there, looking down at his products, touching them, moving them. He opened his mouth to speak, then closed it again. Without saying a word, he began to pack them back into the cupboard. Derby noticed that it was divided by battens, spaced so as to hold each toy in place. Christiansen fitted the last one in, and slid the door shut and bolted it before he straightened up and turned to Derby.

'Com.' He led the way into his day cabin, and waved Derby to a chair. He opened a locker, and brought out two glasses and a bottle of Scotch. He asked Derby:

'You taking vater? Soda?'

'Water, thanks.'

'So.' He took a jug into the bathroom, and brought it back with an inch of water in it. Derby broke the silence.

'Those toys are wonderful. I'd like —' Christiansen shook his head, pushed a glass across the table.

'Drink, Commander.' Derby took it. He understood the toys.

'Captain. To your boys, in Norway.' Christiansen looked up very quickly. His eyes stayed fixed on Derby's as his hand found his own glass and raised it. He tossed it straight back, and Derby did the same, only his had water in it. Christiansen said, flatly:

'That thing I have only drunk for by my own.' He was pouring more whisky, now. 'Vy you think to say it?'

'I was married only a day before I left England. I'd like to have — I, well, Captain, I envy you your children. Wherever they are.' He thought: T.B. – I may never have them. But he had to avoid thinking about himself and his own problem. There'd be time enough for that later, when he could talk to Sheila about it and a doctor they knew, to advise them. . . . He told Christiansen, casually:

'I can imagine how you feel.' Christiansen splashed a little water into his guest's whisky, and stared into his own as he spoke.

'You asking me, Commander, making them toys, what for. I tell you. I starting it for my boys. I know then, they never have the things I am making. My boys are being too old, now, anyway, they never vant them. So I am giving them to this boys' home, Glasgow place. Maybe they are liking them. Say so. But still for my own boys I am making. Von day, I am telling them so . . .' Christiansen seemed to pull himself up, suddenly. He raised his glass.

'Commander, to the boys *you* vill be having!' They drank to that, and immediately the Norwegian poured out more whisky. Derby could already feel that first drink doing him good, and he raised no objections. Suddenly Christiansen leant forward, and stared intensely at his guest.

'Commander, I vish discuss most serious matter.'

32

'Go right ahead.' Christiansen nodded. He shifted forward to the very edge of his chair, and leant over the table. Even that didn't satisfy him: he jerked his head and beckoned, so Derby bent forward, too, until their faces were about an inch apart, above the whisky bottle. Christiansen stared into Derby's eyes: whatever this matter was, it was of dreadful import and no little secrecy.

'Commander!'

'I'm listening, Captain.'

'Commander: is –is comming on boart a vooman!' He flung himself back in his chair so violently that the sudden movement made Derby jump. Christiansen evidently interpreted this as a sign of shock at his announcement.

'Yars, I telling you, Commander! Vot ve do, eh?' Derby raised his eyebrows.

'I personally, Captain, will do absolutely nothing.'

'Ah. You make joke. Bot for me, Commander, is not joking. Vooman in sheep too bad: is making trobbles! I not like this, I very vorry over this vooman, not sleep two night since orders com. I say to bloddy Admiral: "*Vooman?*" I say. "In my *Gangerolf*? Bloddy Hons all right," I say, "bot vooman, this *too moch.*' I say: "Pliss, Admiral, no bloddy voomans!" He say: "Sorry, boy, you got her, you keeping her." You know vot is that Yanky Admiral, Commander?'

'I've met him, once. Seemed quite a decent sort of cove.'

'So. Maybe so. Bot most pighead bloddy Admiral I am ever meeting. Commander —' Christiansen smiled, suddenly. 'You know vot I am hoping?'

'Uh?'

'I am hoping this vooman is gottdam ogly! Sixty year vith vooden leg 'n von eye and balt like coot-bird! You think is possible, Commander? Is ogly beetch, perhaps?' Derby shook his head.

'I'm afraid you're out of luck, Captain. She's about twenty-four years old, five-foot five, perfect figure, dark hair with auburn lights in it. *Lovely* eyes.' He stared at the glowing tip of his Camel cigarette. 'She's – er – very interested in men.'

Christiansen goggled. 'Commander. You are making joke?

You do not know this voomans, you make fonny vith me, huh?'

'Sorry, Captain. I do know her. Her name is Mary Lou, and she's a Wren. A very bright, attractive little Wren.' Christiansen slumped dejectedly in his chair.

'So ... So. Vell, is so.' He stared at his whisky as if he didn't much care for it any more. 'My gott, ve got trobbles now!' Derby tried to cheer him up.

'May not be all that bad, Captain. After all —'

'Commander, is von thing anyvay. This vooman is not officer Wren, I know this. Bot I have only von closs passenger space. She most have cabin by her own, avay from crew, othervise bloddy awful trobbles, eh? You are senior British officer, Commander: is okay she is in firs' closs, eating vith officers?'

'I'm not the senior officer, Captain. My cabin-mate, Lieutenant-Commander Witheringham, is a lot senior to me. But I'm sure he'll agree. Hell, there's really no alternative.'

'Is good fellow, this Witherman?'

'Witheringham. Charming character.' Christiansen sighed. He told Derby:

'Best I spik vith him, I think.' Derby stood up.

'I'll go and tell him you'd like to have a chat. Er – thanks for the whisky, Captain.'

'You are velcom, Commander. Any time you are velcom.' But he spoke tonelessly, without cheer: Derby left him sunk in gloom, morosely contemplating a sea of trobbles.

Derby went cheerfully down to the passenger deck. He liked Christiansen, and felt sorry for him in his strange, almost superstitious fear of women afloat, but at the same time he was considerably brightened by the prospect of what looked to be a highly entertaining voyage. In any case, he felt that the Captain would soon relax when they got under way and he had the navigation of the ship to occupy his mind.

Withers was fast asleep, with his head under the blankets. Derby turned them back, and found a pale face, twitching slightly even in sleep. He took hold of the upper shoulder, and shook it. He spoke loudly.

'Six-thirty, Withers. Time to get up. We're sailing soon, Withers, have to get up. Captain wants to see you, Withers, have to turn out.' Withers didn't open his eyes. But he said, quite clearly:

'*Tell her I haven't got time.*'

Derby stared down at the white profile. He shook the shoulder more violently, and shouted:

'Withers! Turn out! You're late!' Withers opened his eyes. They were pink, like an Angora rabbit's.

'Late? What? Eh? What's that, Derby, late?' Derby sat down on the only chair.

'Captain Christiansen wants to talk to you. Urgently. It's most important.' Withers sat up.

'Why? Why's he want to see *me*?' Derby thought: One might well ask. He told Withers:

'That Wren, Mary Lou. There's no suitable accommodation for her. The Captain says he could put her for'ard, with the crew —'

'Certainly *not*!'

'I'm glad you see it that way. So he suggests I should move out, and sleep in the chart-room, on the settee, so she can move in here, with you. He wants to ask you if you'd mind.'

Wither's eyes were out on stalks. He gripped the edge of the bedclothes and twisted them as if he wanted to tear them up for bandages.

'But – but – it's *preposterous*! Derby! The man must be absolutely *mad*! Derby, is he seriously suggesting that I should – that I – I mean, that Wren Smith —'

'Look, Withers. The Captain wants to see you, that's all. You'd better turn out. He's in his cabin – I'll go up and keep him company. But hurry, won't you?'

III

'He's coming up as soon as he can, Captain.' Derby had found Christiansen leaning on the rail on the starboard side of the boat-deck, dejectedly watching a motor-boat which, still two or three cables off, seemed to be heading for the *Gangerwolf.* Derby asked:

'What time are we sailing?'

'Eight o'clock. Have to vait for bloddy escort. Admiral make us have escort until dark: then ve go alone.' Derby glanced sideways at him.

'Bit risky, isn't it?' Christiansen spat over the side. He said, simply:

'I vill make zigzag like boggery.... Commander, you think the vooman comming, there?' He pointed at the boat, which was much closer and approaching fast.

'Could be.'

Christiansen took a cheroot out of his pocket, and lit it. It smelt like horses being shod. The boat swung almost broadside on, as it began a circle to come alongside *Gangerolf*'s quarter, and at once they could see Mary Lou's small figure in the stern-sheets. She had her cap in her hand so that her hair was blowing out in the wind, and she looked more like an advertisement for Sunny Southsea than a member of His Majesty's Forces.

'That's her, Captain. Shall we go aft, and meet her?' Christiansen thought for a moment. Then he nodded.

'Yars. Othervise maybe she make trobble vith my qvartermaster.' Derby laughed.

'She isn't *that* bad, Captain.'

'You are not knowing my qvartermaster.' Derby followed the big man down to the passenger deck, and they went aft to the ladder where they'd met, an hour ago. The boat was just coming alongside. Christiansen muttered:

'Com.' He shot down the ladder, and headed aft with Derby

just behind him. The quartermaster, the same man who'd received Derby and Withers that afternoon, was clutching the wire guard-rail as if he was electrocuted and stuck to it, and, staring down into the boat, he looked both surprised and pleased. Christiansen roared:

'Kjellegard!' The quartermaster leapt away from the rail, shot a quick look at his bristling Captain, and busied himself with the baggage rope. Christiansen met Mary Lou as she climbed the ladder, and personally assisted her aboard. She gave him one of the smiles she reserved for men who looked promising but had not yet proved themselves. Then, looking past him with her ever-roving eye, she spied Derby.

'Bill, *darling*! How *sweet* of you to meet me!' Christiansen shot a hard look at each of them in turn. For all the bulky Scandinavian charm, he was a man on edge. Derby said quickly:

'Captain, this is – er – Wren – oh, damn it, Mary Lou, what's your surname?' Mary Lou giggled.

'What a *lovely* introduction! I'm Wren Smith, Captain. But everybody *always* calls me Mary Lou. *You* will, *won't* you?' The quartermaster, Kjellegard, suddenly choked. He tried to make it sound like a coughing fit, but Christiansen rounded on him and spoke savagely in Norwegian. Kjellegard, sweating, increased his efforts with Mary Lou's baggage. Behind them, a new voice intruded.

'Ah – er – oh, Derby?' It was Withers, freshly bathed. Derby introduced him.

'Captain, this is Lieutenant-Commander Witheringham. Captain Christiansen.' Christiansen looked relieved.

'Velcom aboart, Commander. Perhaps I have vort with you, von moment?' Withers nodded violently. It was apparent that he was only too anxious to have a word, at the first possible opportunity. Mary Lou smiled at him, but only politely: she didn't like Withers much: he'd stopped her seeing Pompom. Withers bowed slightly. Christiansen asked her and Derby:

'Excuse? Important matter, von moments?' He took Withers by the arm, and they moved for'ard together. Mary Lou looked up at Derby.

'What's up, Bill?'

'Lord knows ... Is this all *your* stuff?' There was certainly a lot more of it than could ever comprise a Wren Rating's regulation kit.

'Yes.' She smiled at the quartermaster. 'Thank you *so* much. Could somebody put it in – well, wherever I'm sleeping?' The quartermaster's eyes rose, slowly and with obvious effort, to her face. He nodded, and turned unwillingly to gather the luggage under his long arms. Derby glanced for'ard, to see whether any sort of decision had been reached. Withers and Christiansen were facing each other: they stood in profile, a dozen yards away, exchanging conversation in low tones. Withers was talking now, in obvious agitation, and suddenly Christiansen interrupted, loudly. They could all hear him, and he sounded angry.

'*Not*, Commander! By gott, *no*!' Withers, looking extremely surprised, took a quick pace backwards, and spoke rapidly in a whisper. Christiansen plainly angry, continued to stare at him. Withers stopped talking, and Christiansen nodded. He said, loudly:

'So ... So! Bot I am votching, Commander, I votch, I stand no bloddy nonsense!'

Derby and Mary Lou looked at each other. Her expression asked for an explanation. He shrugged his shoulders.

'I haven't the slightest idea. Better ask Withers, later on.' The other two were coming back. Christiansen's manner was stern, unbending, and Withers looked both puzzled and upset. The Captain turned sharply to his quartermaster, and pointed at Mary Lou's luggage.

'Nomber two cabin, bloddy qvick!' He told Mary Lou: 'Madame, I give you nomber two cabin. If you have trobble, you ring bell.' He looked at Withers. 'Tell Steward you vish spik vith Captain.' He looked back at Mary Lou, and asked: 'Is onderstood?'

'Why – er – yes, Captain, certainly.' She looked puzzled. 'But why should I – want to complain?'

'Madame. You are the only vooman in this sheep. I am not vishing to be having trobbles. Pliss, follow.' The Captain

38

turned, and stumped for'ard behind the quartermaster, who was carrying most of Mary Lou's luggage. She picked up a small leather cosmetic case, and hesitated, looking at Derby.

'Is he – all right?' Withers broke in with a tense whisper. His face was scarlet, still.

'He's mad! Absolutely mad!' Mary Lou glanced at him, shrugged, patted Derby's hand, and hurried away to catch up with Christiansen. Derby asked Withers:

'What the hell was all that about?' Withers waved his hands helplessly.

'The man's a lunatic, Derby! We were standing there, discussing this thing quietly and calmly, and I'd given my permission for the girl to mess with us, and a second later he started shouting at me in a *most* unpleasant manner. Derby, d'you think he's sane? Has he —'

'What were your last words, before he – er – blew his top?' Withers stared for'ard: he looked dazed. The others had gone from sight, up the ladder to the passenger deck.

'Oh, I'm not sure. Certainly nothing to upset him. He'd said he was going to put her in number two cabin, and – frankly – I was immensely relieved. I realized at once that *you* must have talked him out of that other idea. So I just mentioned it in passing, and he —'

'What were your exact words?'

'Well, something like: "Captain, I've considered the suggestion that she should be accommodated with me, in my cabin, and —" I was going to finish: "and while as senior British officer on board your ship I am anxious to co-operate in every possible way, I do feel that such an arrangement might well be misinterpreted" – something of that sort. But he didn't let me finish, he just —'

'Exploded. 'M.' Derby stared out to sea, and tapped with the tips of his fingers on the top of a guard-rail stanchion. 'Well, I think he's a bit strung up. That's all. Touchy.'

'Now I come to think of it, Derby, he did smell of whisky. It made me feel sick. I think I smoked too much, last night.

'He's worried, old man. Sailing out of convoy, you know – these blokes aren't used to it. Makes 'em feel – naked. And as far as Mary Lou's concerned, these Norwegians are intensely superstitious. One woman in a ship, you know – Jonah, and all that rubbish.'

'Jonah wasn't a woman.'

'Christiansen probably doesn't know that. Norwegians only recognize two kinds of people – seamen, and women.'

They turned, and walked slowly for'ard, side by side. Withers said:

'He must have an extremely undisciplined ship's company, Derby. You know, I suggested that he might put a night sentry outside the girl's door. Know what he said?'

'Of course I don't know.'

'He told me quite seriously that he wouldn't trust any member of his crew within a mile of her door, day *or* night.'

At about seven-thirty, Derby watched life coming to the *Gangerolf*. It came slowly, in dribbles of oddly and scantily-clad Norwegians staggering sleepily out of their quarters and moving, singly and in groups, to their duty stations. Most of them went to the foc'sle, and this seemed natural enough, since the ship was at anchor. Others climbed languidly to the bridge, or to the wheelhouse, and some, appearing at first on deck to gulp fresh air, crept back into the body of the ship and lowered themselves without enthusiasm through hatches above the machinery spaces. Kjellegard slowly hauled in the Jacob's ladder, on the quarter, and rolled it up. Then he shambled for'ard and up ladders to his job in the wheelhouse, where he first of all tested the engine-room telegraphs and then leant with his forehead against the glass windbreak, doing absolutely nothing, which was his favourite occupation. He was a very good quartermaster.

Derby wandered from point to point, watching all of this, deeply interested in the working arrangements of a ship which was neither British nor a warship. The main difference seemed to him to be an almost deliberately casual attitude in every movement, a determined slouch in the individual and an apparent lack of centralize direction in the mass.

A couple of miles out to seaward, two American destroyers were circling, waiting to form up as anti-submarine escort ahead of the Norwegian as soon as he cleared the port. Christiansen, on the side of the bridge, was staring at them through his binoculars, and Derby, watching them, saw also an element of stupidity or at any rate carelessness in such tactics. If he, patrolling in a submarine off an enemy port, spotted escort vessels hanging around outside it, he'd hang around too, to see what they might be waiting for. In fact he'd done that very thing, a couple of years ago, during a patrol off the Italian coast when he'd been operating from Malta. He'd sat quiet and kept an eye on the Italian destroyers – off Crotone, it had been – and the wait had resulted in a most impressive firework display, because the ship that came out at dusk to join her escort had been deep laden with chemicals from the factory there, and the chemicals had reacted splendidly to his torpedoes.

From the wing of the bridge, Christiansen yelled something in Norwegian at his Chief Officer on the fo'c'sle, and a moment later the anchor cable began to clank inboard, each link crashing angrily on the steel deck plate as the capstan dragged it up through the hawse. The cable party on the fo'c'sle stood around in attitudes of weary boredom, and from time to time the Chief Officer swore at them, either to keep them awake or simply as a matter of routine.

Derby went up on deck, and through the passage to the other side, where he found an American army officer leaning on the rail and staring without much expression at the flat and oily surface of the anchorage. Here, on the lee side, you could smell the cable as it rose, wet and muddy. The American turned, and stared at Derby. He was a young man, with close-cropped ginger hair and a pudgy face.

'Hi. You the Captain?'

'No. I'm —'

'Mate, huh. Well, I guess we can't *all* be Captains, huh?' He laughed loudly at that, and slapped Derby on the shoulder. 'Glad t' meet ya, fella. Spatter's the name, Spike Spatter. Captain, U.S. Army.'

Derby shook hands with him.

'How d'you do. I'm not the Mate, though. Passenger. My name is Derby: Lieutenant-Commander, Royal Navy. Are you a passenger?' The American clapped both hands to his belly, and bent almost double, choking with laughter. When he straightened up, he said, short of breath:

'I guess ya could call me that! Yeah, I guess ya could, too!' He began to laugh again, then caught hold of himself. 'That's real humorous, Commander. Fact, I'm looking after a load of Krauts. Fellas off of a U-boat the U.S. Navy sunk. Yessir, them U.S. Navy boys is sure good when it comes t' sinkin'. Just blow 'em out th' water, them fellas do! Knock 'em down in heaps, I'm tellin' ya!' He paused, and looked sideways at Derby. 'Maybe ya knoo?'

'No.' Derby felt he had to be truthful. Years ago, his father had suggested the Diplomatic, as a career. Derby had an idea even then that it wasn't the best idea a father ever had, and quite soon afterwards Derby Senior had accepted the wisdom of his son's doubts. Now Derby told the American: 'No, I hadn't heard ... Tell me, are you alone, in charge of these prisoners?'

Spatter's laughter was too much for him, this time. He had to throw his arms round Derby's shoulders just to hold himself up. A rush of blood darkened his face, and tears streamed out of his eyes. Derby stood quietly in the strange embrace, waiting for the fit to pass. Withers stepped out of the passenger entrance.

'*Good heavens*! ... Are you all right. Derby?'

'Eh?' Derby twisted his head, and saw Withers goggling at him. 'Oh, it's you. Yes, I'm all right. Something I said seems to've amused this chap. His name's Spatter, and he's in charge of the Germans.'

'*Germans*, Derby?'

'Yes, Germans. U-boat prisoners. Some Yank destroyer must've rammed one in error. Anyway, the survivors came aboard while you were snoring.' The American could speak, now.

'Commander, there's near thirty of them Krauts. So natur-

42

ally when you says am I looking after them on my Jack Jones, I think it's funny see?' Withers spoke without thought.

'*Terribly* funny.' The Yank glanced at him, just briefly.

'Hi, fella.' He turned back to Derby. 'I got me a squad numberin' eight, repeat eight, enlisted men down there, keepin' th' Krauts quiet. An' boy, if we Americans ain't knowing how ta keep Krauts quiet, why *nobody* does!' He stared belligerently at Withers, who quickly agreed.

'I dare say you're right, Mr – er —'

'You're goddam right I'm right. Say – you th' Mate?'

'I beg your pardon?'

'That's okay, fella. You the Mate of this tub?' Withers looked offended. Derby apologized.

'I should have introduced you. This, Withers, is Captain Spatter of the American Army. And this, Spatter, is Lieutenant-Commander Witheringham of the Royal Navy.' Spatter curtsied.

'Pleased t' meet ya, Admiral. Folks call me Spike.' Withers said:

'Ah.' He turned to Derby, and asked quietly as though it was a very private matter and certainly didn't concern foreigners: 'Have you any idea where I could get something to drink? I think it might settle my stomach. A bar, of any sort – have you —'

'Must be, old man. There's a steward, anyway. You joining us, Spike?' The American looked pleased, seriously pleased.

'Y' got a plan there, Commander. *I'll* say y' got a plan. Plans is matters Spatter always falls in with, long as they're legal. Spatter never refuses, boy!'

Derby pushed Withers and Spatter through the doorway ahead of him, and turned for a moment to look out at the sea. They were under way, making some fifteen knots, and the Yank destroyers were closing in on the bow. It was a very peaceful thing to look at. Regretfully, he followed the other two into the warm bowels of the ship. He thought: If Spatter never refuses, Spatter isn't going to get asked very often.

They filed along the passage, and into the lounge, and Derby scanned the walls for a bell-push. He found one, and

43

prodded it. After about five minutes, during which time the American and Withers sat staring at their feet and Derby went on periodically pressing the bell, a tall, slim youngster in a white jacket strolled into the lounge and stood there smiling at them. He had wavy blond hair and a way of touching it gently with the tips of his fingers. Derby asked him:

'Are you the steward?' The man giggled. He spoke quite good English, on a falsetto key.

'Alas, sir, no! *I* am the waiter, only!' He giggled again, and Derby frowned.

'What's the difference?'

'The steward, sir, is a *most important* man. The catering, the stores, so many *intricate* matters . . . I, sir, am just his *slave*.'

Withers coughed. Derby said: 'All right, Withers.' He asked the waiter: 'Can you bring us some drinks?'

'But, most *certainly*, sir! What shall —'

'Brandy,' said Withers. He spoke more firmly than he usually did. 'Brandy, and dry ginger ale, and plenty of ice. That's what *I* want, and I want it quickly.'

They all looked at him, surprised at the power of command which he had not previously displayed. The waiter inclined his gleaming, yellow head.

'As you are wishing, sir. And you gentlemen?'

Derby said: 'Scotch and water.' Spatter nodded.

'Scotch here, too. But on the rocks. Get it?' The waiter bowed.

'I am getting it *immediately*, sir.' He smiled shyly at them all, then turned and floated away with his hands dangling rather strangely at his sides. Withers exploded.

'Good God!'

Spatter chuckled, and slapped himself on the knee.

'Y' c'n say *that* again! Hell, Commander, they got 'em most every place, this day 'n age. . . . Don't much care for ass, my-self.' He began to laugh, almost hysterically. Withers gave him a sharp, suspicious glance, then shifted his eyes to Derby and raised his brows. Derby asked Spatter:

'You – er – you've tried it?'

44

'*Tried* it?' Spatter slapped the knee again and shouted: '*Tried* it? Commander, Spatter is a boy tries most ev'rythin' once or maybe more frequent even. But that's one I ain't so far got around to.'

'I thought you said —'

'Manner o' speaking, Commander, just a manner o' speaking.' Withers muttered:

'*A most peculiar one*. Derby, where on earth is that steward?'

'Waiter.'

'Eh?'

'He's a waiter, not a steward.'

'He's an ass-boy,' said Spatter. '*That's* what he is. Say, either you fellas gotta smoke?' Derby brought out his case.

'Withers, smoke?'

'No, thank you. But if that steward isn't here in one minute, Derby, I'm going to make a fuss!'

'You do that, Commander.' Spatter stuck a cigarette into his mouth and patted his pockets. 'Well, whad'ya know – right outa lights, too.' Derby was about to strike a match when he saw Mary Lou framed in the doorway. The others, with their backs that way, couldn't see her. Derby tossed the matchbox to Spatter, and stood up. Spatter leaned over and nudged Withers.

'Here's liquor, Commander. Guess we'll glimpse that ole famous smile again, huh?'

Derby had pulled up a chair between his own and Withers. He told Mary Lou:

'Come and sit down.' Spatter stared at him.

'Well, of all the —'

'Mary Lou, this is Spatter. He's American. Spatter – Miss Smith.' Mary Lou moved sweetly into the room: she was wearing a low cotton frock, and the sound of her high heels tapping the deck was an echo of a distant, half-forgotten world. Spatter, whirling, stared at her with his mouth open and an incredulous expression in his eyes. She smiled at him as she slid into her chair.

'How do you do, Mr Splatter.'

'Huh? Oh yeah! I – well, see, I kinda thought it was that waiter guy, see, else I'd a' – well, I'd —'

'You're – disappointed, Mr Splatter?'

'Huh? Oh hell, I – I guess *not*!' He began to scream with laughter, then stopped abruptly and sat down. 'Jees!' He went on staring at her, with his mouth open, and she turned to the others.

'I thought it'd be better for me to wear civvies. I mean, in an officers' mess —'

'Quite right.' Withers nodded violently, but his eyes were on the tray of drinks which the waiter was just setting down. 'You were absolutely right. This is my brandy? Eh? Why've you put so much ice in it, steward?'

'That is whisky, sir. For *this* gentleman. Your brandy is *here*.' Withers stretched a shaky hand towards it, and the waiter gave Spatter the bill. Derby asked Mary Lou:

'What'd you like to drink, Mary Lou?'

'Oh, anything. Gin and tonic'd be lovely.' The waiter bowed.

'Gin and tonic water for Madame. *Immediately*.' He slid out, and Spatter sat there staring at the bill instead of Mary Lou.

'Hell, Commander, I guess I thought —'

'Give me that.' Derby took it from him. Withers was splashing ginger ale into his brandy; he asked Mary Lou:

'Do you mind if I don't wait? Terribly thirsty, I don't know why. Cheers.' Derby told her:

'Withers has a headache. Too much pompom, last night.' She laughed, and Spatter jerked upright in his chair. He pointed at Withers, and asked Derby:

'Pompom? *Him?*' Derby shrugged his shoulders, and Spatter slowly subsided. 'Well, I'll be – *well*!' Mary Lou said:

'You're getting a *lot* of surprises today, Mr Splatter.' The American nodded slowly.

'Yeah. I guess *so*.' Withers was lying back, sipping his drink: he had his eyes closed, and occasionally a long sigh escaped him. Plainly, at this moment he cared little for the world outside his own small sufferings.

On *Gangerolf*'s bridge, Captain Christiansen stared into the gathering dusk, and gave some angry thought to Withers. The man had behaved atrociously, and Christiansen had half-a-mind to make an official report of the matter. If it had been Derby, or the Chief Officer, or even the Quartermaster, he'd have understood it. Prevented it, of course, in the interests of keeping order on board his ship, but still he wouldn't have been surprised or shocked: there'd be nothing unusual or horrifying in a normal, healthy male making a pass at an attractive young woman. (He thought: A *very* attractive young woman!) Especially in this climate, and a womanless society. He himself, if it wasn't that he was the captain and therefore responsible for setting an example to the rest of them, might have been tempted to show more than mere courtesy to the girl. But that elderly weasel, that dried-out cockroach Witherham, that he should use his position as senior British officer to try and force a girl young enough to be his daughter into actually *sharing his cabin*, that, *that*, thought Christiansen, glaring fiercely at an American destroyer three cable lengths out on *Gangerolf*'s port bow, was foul, indecent, and profoundly disturbing to the mind of an honourable man.

Christiansen decided that he would show his disapproval by refusing to speak to Witherham at any time during the voyage. And what was more, he'd have the man watched, closely, day and night. Relieved at having come to this decision, the Captain paced slowly across to the other side of the bridge, and leant there in the starboard wing. The American escort on this side had dropped out of station: she wasn't more than two cables off, perhaps one and a half. As Christiansen watched her, a light began to flash from her bridge, calling *Gangerolf*. Christiansen roared for his signalman, and when the man appeared, took the opportunity to ask him whether he'd lost the use of his eyes. Without answering, the signalman grabbed an Aldis lamp and flashed acknowledgement to the American. The American came over slowly, dots and dashes bright yellow in the growing night: a mist of darkness hung over the smooth swell of sea, and the only sounds were the swish of it along the ship's side and the occasional clack of the lamp's trigger as the signalman acknowledged the Yank's message, word by word. When it was complete, he stowed the lamp in its rack and turned in to the wheelhouse to write it down quickly before it went out of his mind. Christiansen followed him inside, and read the massage over the man's shoulder:

We are scheduled to return to harbour now. Will you be all right on your own?

Christiansen crossed over to the open window on the lee side, and spat through it. He turned to the signalman.

'Tell him to bogger off.' The signalman nodded, and started for the door. Christiansen said:

'Hey, vait.'

'Huh?' The signalman, who was an Australian, paused, looking at the Captain over his shoulder.

'Say, *Good-bye, thankings*.' Christiansen moved up to the binnacle. Kjellegard still had the wheel, and he was two-and-a-half degrees off course. The Captain, as a matter of form, asked him where the hell he thought he was taking them all to: Kjellegard nodded, and shifted his hands slightly on the spokes of the wheel. Satisfied, the Captain moved out on to the bridge, where the signalman had just taken a farewell message from the escort.

'He said, *Good luck*, Cap'n.'

Christiansen's eyebrows rose. *Good luck*, indeed! Perhaps Americans used luck, but he had been trained to rely on seamanship. So far, it hadn't failed him. He leant against the windbreak and watched the destroyers' dim shapes slip away into the wall of dark: now, *Gangerolf* was alone. He thought: Perhaps a little luck may be of value, too, this trip. There was a long way to go, and Jap submarines still hunted in these waters: well, they wouldn't catch his *Gangerolf*. He pushed into the wheelhouse, and called the Chief Engineer on the intercom.

'Engineer speaking.'

'Chief. I want another two – three knots.'

'You can't have them.'

The Captain's face darkened, and he scowled at the receiver in his hand.

'That is an order. I shall call for increased revolutions in five minutes' time.'

'The engines won't stand it.'

'They'll bloody well have to!'

'What about fuel consumption?' The Captain rang off. That engineer was a good technician, and a pleasant fellow too, away from his engines. But at times like this, he was an old woman. A *grumpy* old woman. Sometimes the Captain wondered if his engineer had some dash of Swedish blood in him: but he told himself quickly: No, that's unfair: that's going too far. He's just a pig-headed old fool, that's all.

The Chief Officer lurched into the wheelhouse and flicked a cheerful salute at his Captain.

'All's secure, sir.'

'Eh? Oh good. Good. Come out here, Olafson. Want a word with you.' Christiansen led the Mate out on to the dark bridge, right out to the wing, where nobody'd hear them talking.

'Listen. You'll know, there's a woman passenger. That's bad enough. What's worse, there's a fellow called Witherham – the *worst* king of Englishman. A thoroughly unpleasant character —'

'Is he the little skinny one with a white face and pop eyes?' Christiansen frowned, and nodded.

'That's him. Why – have you —'

'He's getting drunk, down there. I looked into the lounge for a minute, and he's lying on the back of his neck swallowing litres of brandy and not saying a word to anyone. The others aren't taking any notice of him. I was going to mention it —'

'So!' The Captain's eyes flashed angrily in the half-dark. 'A drunk, too! Well, if necessary, I'll stop his liquor. And in any case, Olafson, I want him watched, all round the clock. Can you spare a reliable man?'

Olafson scratched his head, thoughtfully. 'The Carpenter's Mate, sir? He's on Light Duty, since he sprained his wrist. He's not much use to me.'

'How'd he do that?'

The Mate shrugged. 'They tell me he hit the Carpenter.'

'So? Why?'

'Lord knows. I suppose he got fed up with him.' The Mate asked: 'What orders shall I give him, sir?'

The Chief Officer presided over dinner in the saloon, but his knowledge of English was extremely limited, and very little conversation was exchanged between him and the passengers. Periodically he nodded and smiled at Mary Lou, but far more frequently he darted quick, suspicious looks at Withers. Now and then, he offered Derby a plate of cheese, and at each time of offering Derby smiled as pleasantly as he could and murmured:

'No thanks, old man. I'll have some later, though.' The Chief Officer ate cheese all the time, with every course.

Withers said nothing at all to anybody. He refused soup, swallowed a few mouthfuls of fish, discarded a plate of some sort of Irish Stew after giving it only one highly critical stare, then, just after he'd eaten a small piece of cheese which the Chief Officer had been almost begging him to accept, he flung his chair back and rushed out of the room. The Chief Officer stared after him, and slowly nodded.

'So!' Derby said, quickly:

'I'm afraid Commander Witheringham is rather unwell. Something he ate yesterday upset him.' The Chief Officer beamed delightedly, and passed the cheese: it seemed he thought Derby had asked for it. Spatter said:

'Say – er – excuse me, Miss – er – Smith.' He leaned across her, and spearing a piece of cheese on the end of his knife, transferred it directly from the knife to his mouth. He chewed loudly, with his mouth open, and he spoke at the same time.

'Say, Commander, you're missin' somethin'! This cheese they got is real good!'

Derby told him: 'From here, it looks real awful.'

After dinner, Derby found himself alone with Mary Lou, on the boat-deck. She had her arm in his, and they were leaning on the rail, in a gap between the second and third boats on the starboard side. Derby was at peace, enjoying the idea that up there on the bridge other men were responsible for the safety of the ship and the working of her routine: there was something very pleasant in being a passenger, and particularly in being one in a ship homeward bound. After such a long time, it seemed almost too good to be true. They'd cure the T.B. thing, he was sure: nowadays, they could cure anything.

Mary Lou whispered:

'The moonlight's wonderful, isn't it?' Her voice was very clear, beside him, but he didn't really hear it.

'Eh? What did you say? I'm —'

'On the water. The moon.'

'Oh. Yes, it is, isn't it. I'm afriad I was —'

'Miles away!' She had twisted round with her back against the rail, looking up at him. 'Where were you, Bill?'

'Oh – home. My wife. That sort of thing.'

'She's very good-looking, isn't she?'

'Well – yes, she is. Very. What *is* this, Mary Lou?'

'Nothing. Just conversation. It's a thing people make, and I'm inquisitive, too. Sorry if I —'

'Don't be an idiot.' His mind still wasn't on this. She let go of his arm.

'I – I think I'll go and read a bit. I can't ever do it for long, though: it puts me to sleep, just a page or two and I'm out.' He asked her, as she moved away:

'What are you reading? The Seamanship Manual?' She laughed.

'Nothing so exciting. I —' She was back again, her hand on his arm. 'Bill, we could have fun. Nobody'd know. Mummy had an old char once, and one of her favourite sayings was, "What the eye don't see, the 'eart don't grieve for". Bill, if the 'eart don't grieve, what —'

Derby laughed. He couldn't help it. Mary Lou caught her breath, and asked him:

'You're amused?'

'Oh, for heaven's sake! ... Yes, I am. This never happened to me before. I feel I ought to say: "I'm not that sort of boy"!'

51

'Why don't you?'

'Look, Mary Lou. I'm married. And —'

She was gone: just the tapping of her high heels and the crash of the swing door, and he was alone in the dark between the boats. He waited until she'd have had time to get to her cabin, then he went in to find himself a drink. A large one, without much water. In fact – and the thought brightened him – he'd have it Spatter's way. *On the rocks.*

At about half-past three in the morning, Withers awoke. Even at the moment of waking, he was aware of great physical discomfort: his head ached, he felt sick, and he was suffocating. Above all, he wanted fresh air. He was lying on his right side, facing the bulkhead: now he rolled over on to his other side, to face into the cabin, and at once he wished that he'd stayed as he was, because the movement had disturbed his stomach and considerably increased the sensation and threat of nausea. Sweat pricked the skin of his face, and in sudden panic he struggled out of the bunk and began to grope about on the floor for his slippers. Unable to locate them, he gave up the search, and, with his hands held out in front of him, blindly sought the door. By now he was quite certain that he was going to be sick.

His outstretched hands passed the corner of the steel wardrobe, but the rest of him hit it. The impact jarred him from head to toe, although it had seemed to him that he was moving slowly. He recoiled, biting his tongue, but sheer necessity drove him forward again: the clang of his knee and forehead striking the cold metal still echoed in his ears, and there was fresh, sharp pain at those points, but this was nothing compared to the overpowering discomfort from within. He was damp with sweat, and struggling for air.

His hands found the switch, easily enough, and he flicked on the lights. Gasping with pain and exhaustion, he seized the handle of the door, dragged it open, and stepped out into the dimly-lit corridor. Into a stream of cooler air, into the hum and throb of machinery: the lavatory, he knew, was only a dozen paces away, just around the other corner. He stepped out into the corridor, and it seemed to Withers that the doors of Hell had closed behind him. But he'd reckoned without the Carpenter's Mate.

'Not, pliss!'

Startled, Withers looked up and found himself confronted by a huge Norwegian who had one of his arms in a sling and the other raised as though signalling traffic to halt. Withers gaped.

'What?'

'Beck, pliss. In cabin.' The large man spoke with an air of authority. Withers tried to ignore him, to pretend that this was not really happening at all. He tried to pass by, but the fellow side-stepped too, and repeated more loudly:

'Beck!' Withers stared angrily up at him.

'What the devil d'you mean, *Beck*?'

The man pointed over Withers's shoulder, and shuffled slowly forwards so that Withers had no choice but to move backwards. His stomach heaved, and his head span. In sudden panic he yelled at the madman:

'I'm going to be sick!' The other nodded, mulishly.

'So. In cabin, pliss.' He reached past Withers, and opened the cabin door: it swung inwards, and he tried to manoeuvre Withers into it by swinging at him with the elbow of his damaged arm. Out of sheer desperation, Withers had a brainwave: he whirled round, and rushed aft down the corridor. The Norwegian pounded heavily after him, shouting commands or imprecations in his own language. Withers, terrified, increased speed: he flung himself through the door at the after end of the passage, down the ladder, across the officers' sun-deck to the other ladder and so up into the port side of the passenger deck. A moment later, he had locked himself in the lavatory.

Presently, weak and very cold, he cautiously unlocked the door and peered out. The Norwegian was standing a few paces away, grinning. Withers tried to assume an air of affronted dignity.

'I wish to return to my cabin.'

'Beck?' The man seemed calmer, at any rate less hostile.

Withers stepped past him, then stopped and said as firmly as he could:

'I shall make a full report of your behaviour in the morning, to the Captain.' Keenly aware that the lunatic was following close behind, he resumed his progress down the passage. He could almost feel the man's hot breath on the back of his neck, and he walked stiffly, in dread of a sudden blow from the rear: he stalked all the way to his cabin without once looking back, in case any display of anxiety should provoke some fresh assault.

The cabin door was open, and the light was on. Withers approached it slowly, then sprang in, slammed the door and shot the bolt. From the top bunk came Derby's sleepy voice:

'What an awful racket you're making, Withers! Do put the light off.'

IV

Derby stood naked at the small wash-basin, working up a lather on his cheeks. He was enjoying it, because for once there wasn't any hurry: a day to pass, and nothing to do in it except eat and talk and have a drink or two, read something, perhaps take an afternoon nap. It was worth getting up for. He was just about to apply the razor, when Withers, who to this moment had shown no sign of life, groaned and stirred. Derby, razor in hand, turned and saw that the man was not only alive, but awake.

'Morning, Withers.' There was no reply, only that pale, anxious stare, so he turned back to the mirror and went ahead with the shaving. When he'd finished, and washed the soap off his ears, he found that Withers had turned over and was facing the wall.

'Withers!' The head twitched slightly, as though it had tried to turn but failed in the attempt. 'Withers?'

'Yes?' The voice was weak, dispirited.

'Last night, or this morning – some unmentionable time, anyway – you woke me up and said something about being assaulted in the lavatory. Didn't you?' Withers rolled over.

'You said, "Nonsense", and laughed, and went back to sleep. Yes, you did! But it's true, a madman, an enormous foreigner with a – a —'

'Start from the beginning, old man. I've only the vaguest recollection—' Withers sat up, moved by his own excitement.

'Just outside this door! I wasn't feeling at all well, in fact I was ill, really ill. I wanted to get to the heads. But as soon as I opened the door, there he was! Shouting at me, and trying to hit me. He wanted to force me back in here! I got round the other way, and when I came out he was still hanging about and he followed me all the way back. Honestly, Derby, if I hadn't kept my head and my presence of mind he'd have done me a serious injury, I'm sure of it!'

Derby was pulling on his shorts. He asked:

'What did this – this creature look like?'

'Norwegian. About six-foot-six, and powerfully built. He had one arm in a sling. I'm certain he must be a lunatic, Derby, I'm going to see the Captain —'

'Oh no?' Derby shook his head slowly. 'No, Withers, old man. I wouldn't do that, if I were you. Really I wouldn't.'

'Damn it, why not? D'you think I'm going to let a raving lunatic chase me about the ship in the middle of the night, and get away with it? Eh? What d'you think I felt like?'

'Pretty spare, I should imagine. But if you go to the Captain with that yarn, he'll have you locked up.'

'Locked up? Derby, are you insane? Why on earth —'

'He'll think *you're* insane, old man. That's why . . . Look, *I* know you. I know you believe it all, and naturally you're very upset about it. But the more upset you are, the more – well, unbalanced, you might seem to be. And frankly, old man, it can only have been a nightmare. One of those highly realistic —'

'I *didn't* dream it!' Withers, ridiculous in his agitation and his striped pyjamas, sprang out of the bunk and clutched Derby's arm. 'I tell you it *happened*! It happened to *me*, Derby, I was *there*, I *know*! You *must* believe me!' He turned, and pointed dramatically at the door. 'There! Just outside! *That's* where he was!' Derby sat down on a suitcase, and began to tie the laces of his shoes.

'Withers, old man. Take it easy. If I was the Captain, and you came bounding up waving your arms like that, and telling me all that stuff about being assaulted and lavatories and presence of mind – well, frankly I'd have no doubts at all. I'd say you were off your rocker.'

'Derby —'

'Yes. And for your own safety, I'd lock you up.' Withers sat down on the edge of his bunk. He looked so unhappy that Derby really felt very sorry for him. Withers muttered:

'I suppose it does sound – strange. . . . But imagine how I felt, Derby, when I opened that door and an enormous sailor started up out of the dark and – Derby, I can't just *ignore* it! I must do *something*! Suppose it happened again!'

'I'm sure that's most unlikely. It's still real to you now: a nightmare like that can be an awful shock to the system, I know. But it'll wear off.'

'This was not a nightmare, Derby.' Withers was keeping his voice steady with obviously conscious effort. 'It happened to me, while you were asleep. It was when I came back into the cabin, and banged the door shut, that I woke you. The noise of the door —' Derby nodded.

'All right. I don't believe it, old man, but just for the sake of argument let's imagine it's true, and you shoot along to our pal Christiansen and tell him that one of his men is a nut and tried to stop you using the lavatory. Look – in the first place, he won't believe you. In the second place, d'you remember how he suddenly rounded on you, yesterday? For no reason at all?'

Withers was silent. Derby told him: 'If I were you, old man, I'd forget the whole thing.'

Breakfast consisted largely of cold meat and cheese. Derby and Spatter, facing each other across the table, ate it in silence, under the waiter's watchful gaze. When he'd finished, Derby helped himself to a third cup of coffee, and asked the waiter:

'Has Miss Smith had her breakfast yet?' The waiter slipped him a quick smile.

'Oh yes, sir. But only coffee with marmalade, on a tray in her cabin.' Spatter looked surprised. He told Derby: 'I never had coffee with marmalade. Sugar 'n' cream for Spatter.' Derby thought: Arsenic for Spatter. He asked:

'And the Chief Officer?'

'He is on watch, sir.'

'Ah. The Captain?'

'The *Captain*, sir? Oh, Captain Christiansen *never* comes down here, when the vessel is at sea. I carry his foods to him, on trays.' Spatter, with his mouth full, commented:

'Wouldn't do in buckets, I'd dare say.' Derby told the waiter:

'You'd better take some coffee to Commander Witheringham, in cabin three.'

'Only coffee, sir? The Commander is unwell?' Derby said, firmly:

'Just take him some black coffee.' The waiter coughed.

'Perhaps I should inform him, sir, if he is not yet rising, that there will be lifeboat drill at ten o'clock?'

Captain Christiansen enjoyed eating, and one of the privileges of Command which he most appreciated was that of taking his meals alone. He had never been a 'passenger Captain' – and if, after the war they tried to make him into one, well, he'd already made up his mind that he'd resign and join a tanker company. Once it had happened that a passenger whom he liked had persuaded him to take dinner in the saloon, and Christiansen had hated every minute of it. He had been forced to make light conversation when there was nothing he wished to say, to pass plates of things to and fro when anyone at the small table could quite easily have grabbed what they wanted without any fuss at all, and to smile at people he didn't much like when his mouth was already so full that bending it into a smile was practically impossible. So nowadays the waiter had standing instructions that when any passengers asked about the Captain coming down for meals, he was to tell them, if the ship was at sea, that the Captain always had meals in his cabin at sea, or if the ship was in port, that the Captain never took meals in the saloon in harbour.

Christiansen ate noisily. He'd tuck a napkin into his collar so that his uniform would not suffer too heavily from spillage, and once he'd started eating he'd carry on doing that and nothing else until either he was too full to eat any more, or there was nothing left to eat. In the latter case, if time permitted, he'd send down for more.

But now, there wasn't time for more, and in any case he'd just about touched the capacity-mark, He'd started with porridge, moved on to fried eggs with tinned sausages, and then cleaned up a plate of cold meat and sweetcorn. A little bread and cheese, washed down by several cups of coffee, rounded off the first snack of the day. He burped, pushed his chair back from the table, and lit a Dutch cheroot. It didn't draw as well as it should have, so he dropped it into the dregs of his coffee and lit another. He sat there blowing thick smoke at the deckhead: the scuttles were full of nothing but clear blue sky, the throb of the engines was easy and regular, a minimum of vibration even at something not far off maximum revolutions. In general, Captain Christiansen was at peace. He removed the cheroot from his lips, and burped a second time: he smiled, then, as he watched a perfect smoke-ring drift lazily across the cabin.

But all good moments end, and now, glancing at the electric clock on the bulkhead, he saw that it was time for him to put in an appearance on the bridge. In half an hour, it would be ten o'clock, boat-drill. Uttering a sigh, he rose and stretched. At the same moment there was a knock on the door, and the bridge messenger stuck his head into the cabin. Christiansen lowered his arms.

'Well?'

'Signal, Captain.' The man handed over a folded sheet of paper, and stood there, staring.

'Good. Go.'

'Sir.' The fellow looked disappointed, as if he'd been hoping that he'd be asked to stay for a cup of coffee, or a discussion of the signal He stumbled noisily out of the cabin, and clattered up the stairway to the bridge. Christiansen opened the signal, and saw at once that it was a submarine report. Enemy submarine – surfaced – position, and a time of sighting. The Captain shrugged his broad shoulders: offhand, the figures of the position didn't tell him much. But it must be somewhere in their area: better go along and put it on the chart. Not that you could really take much notice of these enemy reports, particularly when they came from aircraft, and American aircraft at that: the 'submarine' might be a floating box, or, if it *was* a submarine, the position would be at least fifty miles out.

Still, one day it could happen that there'd be an accurate one, and this could be it. Christiansen, signal in hand, strolled into the chart-room, stuck the cheroot in the corner of his mouth, and picked up a pencil and the parallel ruler.

A minute later, the cheroot stub burnt his lips: he turned and spat it out, flattened it with his heel. Then for a third time he checked the position of the little cross which he'd marked on the chart. There was no error: it was right where he'd put it, smack on the *Gangerolf*'s mean course, about six hours' steaming, dead ahead. It had been sighted, according to the signal, less than an hour ago. Christiansen climbed slowly to the bridge. He was thinking: Why don't they give a course? Can't they see which way the bloody thing's pointing? It was, in fact, useless information, without an enemy course. If the submarine (granted it was a submarine) was travelling on the surface, it could be making seventeen, eighteen knots. And whichever way *Gangerolf* turned could be the wrong way, because any reasonable alteration could take her to wherever the enemy could by then have settled himself down to wait.

Christiansen leant on the windbreak at the front of the bridge, and wondered what purpose anyone could have intended that signal to serve. He crumpled it into a ball in his pocket, and nodded cheerfully at the Chief Officer.

'Morning, Olafson.'

'Morning, sir. You saw the signal I sent down? About the submarine? Right ahead?'

'Steaming across our course at eighteen knots. So what?' The Mate looked stunned.

'Across our — I didn't see —'

'What course did you read?'

'I – well, I —' Christiansen grinned. The Mate stammered: 'I don't remember exactly, but —'

'Don't worry, Olafson. It's very likely a hundred bloody miles off. More, by now.' He thought: Or it could have just been sitting on the surface and now it's dived, right where they saw it. Perhaps I'd better alter, just for the sake of the record. To satisfy the Admirals. He told the Mate: 'I'll be back presently,' and he went down to the chart-room and stared at the little cross for a minute. He was thinking not of the things he lived by, common sense and seamanship, but of the things he'd seen in the last couple of years, Convoy Conferences and Post Mortems and Planning Sections and private interviews with Chiefs of Staffs. Just for the sake of the record, he thought: There's no damn point in it, it's hit or miss either way, but it'll square my yardarm if there's an Inquiry. But he stood looking down at the new pencil line which he'd just drawn on the chart, a course to clear the little crosses by thirty miles, and he thought: All of that extra distance is wasted steaming time, wasted fuel. Suddenly he thought: I've been working with Americans for too long.

Carefully he rubbed out that new course, and, straightening, spoke aloud to the empty chart-room:

'*Bogger* the record!'

'I wonder how long they're going to keep us standing here.' Wither's plaintive voice irritated Derby. He'd been wondering the same thing himself, and had no answer for it. The waiter had directed them to their lifeboat station, which was abreast the third boat on the port side, and they'd been standing there looking at each other for more than half an hour. Their party consisted of Derby, Withers, Mary Lou, the waiter and a large group of Norwegians, most of whom seemed to be stokers. This was quite likely, too, since the waiter had told them, a few minutes ago, that the Chief Engineer was nominally in charge of this boat. The waiter had added that the Chief Engineer never attended boat-drill, since he considered it a waste of time. Derby nodded.

'I'm with the old boy on that one.' Withers had other objections.

'It seems very odd to me,' he said, 'that an engineer should be in charge of a sea-boat. He's not an executive officer, after all. I think I shall take charge myself.' Derby looked at him sharply.

'You?' Withers seemed affronted by the question.

'I'm the senior officer, aren't I?'

61

'You can't talk Norwegian.'

'What's that got to do with it?'

'How on earth can you take charge if you can't make yourself understood?' Withers waved his hand impatiently.

'I expect some of them talk English. They must have schools. Anyway, I can make signs to them.' Derby laughed.

'Can you see them sitting in a small boat in the middle of the ocean with their eyes fixed on you just in case you might want to make *signs* at them? They aren't interested in your seniority – they expect orders from their own officers.'

'From an engineer?'

'Apparently.'

'It's preposterous!' Mary Lou yawned. She said:

'I think it's silly anyway, making us stand here all day. We aren't doing anybody any good.' Withers glared at her, and she shrugged her shoulders.

There was a similar group opposite each of the other five boats, but they'd drifted into each other and no sort of order was apparent. The men lounged about, or sat on the deck, talking, smoking or sucking sweets. None of them were complaining: presumably they had grown used to spending their forenoons in this way. Withers suddenly perked up, and looked around.

'Derby. I don't see Spatter. Where's Spatter?' Derby strolled over to the starboard side, and looked about. He came back shaking his head.

'Can't see him. Having a nap, perhaps.' Mary Lou said:

'He must have more sense than I thought. Let's *all* go.'

'Certainly not!' The suggestion had angered Withers. He called: 'Waiter!' The waiter ran lightly forward, smiling eagerly.

'You require me, sir?'

'No. I want to know where Captain Spatter is. The American Officer. Didn't you tell him about this drill?'

'Oh yes, sir! He is with the other American gentlemen, with the German prisoners. That is his station, sir.'

'Oh. I see. Very good.'

Withers was certainly seeing himself as officer in charge,

even if nobody else was. He dismissed the waiter with a curt nod.

Mary Lou asked: 'Don't they give prisoners boats? Do they have to swim?' Withers frowned.

'Don't be ridiculous.' He turned his back on her. Derby said:

'Look! Something's happening.' There was a stir, up for'ard, the men who had been lying about were struggling to their feet and falling into lines. The Captain appeared, walking slowly aft, glaring at the men as he passed them and occasionally saying something over his shoulder to the Chief Officer, who followed with a board in his hands. There were papers pinned to the board, and he was counting the men and ticking off names. When eventually the inspection party came to the third boat, Christiansen removed his cap and bowed to Mary Lou. She smiled at him.

'Good-morning, Captain.'

'Madame. All is vell?'

'Lovely, thank you.'

'I am pliss.' He glanced at Withers, but this was quite plainly a mistake, because he immediately looked away again. Seeing Derby, he beamed.

'Morn, Commander. All goot?' Derby saluted.

'All fine, Captain, thank you.' Withers stepped forward, between Derby and the Captain. He was much smaller than either of them.

'Captain! As Senior British Off —' Christiansen had turned his back, and was speaking in loud Norwegian to the Chief Officer, who replied even more loudly. Still talking, they moved over to the next boat, the after one on the starboard side. Withers was scarlet, stammering with rage.

'Derby! D-did you s-see that? Th-th-that —'

'What, Withers? See what?'

'That d-deliberate insult! He turned his b-b-back on me, when I was t-t-talking to him!' Derby looked puzzled.

'Oh, I'm sure you're mistaken. He was turning to speak to the Chief Officer, just when you started talking. I'm sure he

63

couldn't have heard you, old man, really.' The waiter sidled up.

'We may dismiss now, sirs.' He gave Withers an arch smile. 'The bar is open in a few jiffies, sir!' Derby grinned at Withers.

'You seem to've acquired a reputation, old man.' Withers didn't answer: he just walked away, as silent and reserved as a first-class carriage. Derby turned to Mary Lou.

'How about a snifter?' The girl had been quiet, almost shy, all morning, and he wanted to break the ice before it set in really thick. The boat-deck was emptying fast, like the end of break in a school yard. Mary Lou took his arm, and he thought: Whatever else, she has some sense. She said, happily:

'Can't think of anything I'd like more.'

Christiansen leant against the front of the bridge, and, raising his binoculars, adjusted their focus to the line of the horizon. He examined it carefully, sweeping from one bow to the other and back again. It was clear, but the nagging worry remained in his mind, and he called to the officer of the watch:

'Eriksen! Come here.' Eriksen, the Second Officer, was a Dane. He came over quickly, and flipped a hand to the peak of his cap.

'Sir?'

'Some time ago there was a report of a submarine ahead of us. See the Look-outs don't slack, boy.'

'Aye aye, sir.' Christiansen grunted, and crossed over to the other side of the bridge. In the wing, the starboard Look-out had his glasses at his eyes, slowly sweeping the quarter. Christiansen felt an urge to tell the man to concentrate on the bow, but he restrained himself. An all-round look-out, that was the essential: attack could come from any quarter, and more likely from the beam than from anywhere. It was only that he had at the back of his mind a focus on that small pencilled cross, right in *Gangerolf*'s track. He was also uncomfortably

64

aware that submarines were harder to see, even on the surface, than surface ships, and in general had the reputation of keeping better look-outs than anyone else.

Christiansen faced aft, and glanced up at the streamlined funnel: a long streak of grey smoke trailed from it like a pendant. Not much, but enough to be seen a long way off. He called the officer of the watch over again, and pointed at the smoke.

'Tell the engine-room to stop it.'

'Aye aye, sir.' Eriksen went into the wheel-house, just as the helmsman was putting the wheel over for another leg of the zigzag. There was an alarm clock that buzzed whenever it was time to alter course, and a diagram of the zigzag pattern in a frame just in front of the helmsman. From the helmsman's point of view, it was better than steering a straight course, because it broke the monotony of the four-hour trick. As Eriksen rang the engine-room, he thought: The old boy's nervy, all right. We couldn't make much less smoke than that, however hard we tried. He told the engineer on watch:

'You're making too much smoke.' Another telephone buzzed, so he hung up this one and grabbed the second. 'Bridge.'

'Wireless office here. Messenger for a signal, please.' Eriksen shouted:

'Messenger! Wireless office, quick!' The messenger shot down the ladder. In a moment he was back, and Eriksen took the signal out to the Captain.

'Signal, sir.' Christiansen had his glasses up, staring out over the bow.

'Eh?'

Eriksen repeated: 'A signal, Captain.'

'Oh.' Christiansen dropped the glasses on their lanyard. 'What is it?' He took it out of the Second Officer's hand, and opened it. Another enemy report: aircraft on an A/S sweep had attacked a surfaced submarine, which had then dived. The position, he saw, at a glance, couldn't be far from the earlier one. He nodded to Eriksen, as if the matter was of only casual interest, and strolled across to the ladder.

When he'd put the new position on the chart, he stood and stared at it for a full minute while he made up his mind. It was about fifteen miles away from the first cross, and still dead on their own course. It looked as if the submarine was travelling in the same direction as *Gangerolf*, at about six knots. Fifteen miles, and an interval of about two and a half hours between the sightings. In a few hours, if the enemy held that course and speed, *Gangerolf* would come up astern of him. And with the two reports so close, confirming each other, they couldn't be ignored.

Christiansen worked at the chart for a few minutes. Then he noted the deck-watch time, climbed to the bridge, and told the officer of the watch:

'Alter mean course forty-five degrees to starboard. Start the zigzag again on the hour.'

'Aye aye, sir.' Eriksen glanced at the clock: it showed four minutes to noon. He told the helmsman: 'Steer the mean course.'

Derby leant forward and dropped an ice-cube into Mary Lou's John Collins. She told him:

'More, please. I'm feeling quite tight already. More ice before I start swinging on the chandelier.'

'I'd love to see that ... Oh Lord. Here's Spatter.' The American let the swing door crash behind him, and he raised his right hand in a sort of slovenly Nazi salute.

'Hi, folks. Drinking?'

'No,' said Derby. 'No. Where've you been all day, Spatter?'

'All day? *That* late? What's about th' hour, Commander?'

'Noon. Want a drink?' The American grinned, and dropped into a chair.

'Well, I guess that would be nice. Yeah, I guess so. Say, d'ya know what?'

'What?'

'I lost my watch. Goddam enlisted men took it off me. Finest watch I ever did have, too. Whad'ya think o' that, Miss?'

Mary Lou took a long drink, and set her glass down. 'I think it sounds very odd. Can't you make them give it back?' Spatter shook his head.

'Don't reckon they'd do that. Not *that* circus. Mean as hell. Fact is, though, I lost it fair 'n square, playin' crap. I tell ya, them guys cleaned me out!' Derby pressed the bell. He said:

'Perhaps you'd better not play with them again.' Spatter shrugged.

'Guess I ain't likely to. Got nothin' left to stake. They cleaned me good, them fellers.' The waiter came in, and Derby indicated Spatter. The waiter asked him:

'Yes, sir?'

'Well, Commander, I guess this is mighty generous.' He asked the waiter: 'Got any beer, feller?'

'Australian beer, sir. Black Horse.'

'Okay, boy. Gimme one o' them.' The waiter withdrew. 'Mighty generous, Commander.' Mary Lou told him:

'You were very lucky, not having to come to boat-drill. We had to stand there for hours.'

'That so? Well, Miss, I guess if I'd been along too, I'd still be wearin' a watch on this arm.' Derby asked him:

'Where's your station, Spatter?' Spatter looked grim.

'Now there's a question, Commander. Ya know what?'

'Hardly.'

'Me – my bunch – we don't get no boats. No, sir! D'ya know what we get? Well, I'll tell ya. *Rafts.* Maybe a dozen of 'em, up there on th' back end. They got round tops like motor-tyres only bigger, 'n hard, 'n just a coupla strips o' timber cross th' bottom. I guess they ain't the last word in luxurious-ness, them rafts we got.'

'Carley floats?'

'Maybe. They're like I said. I sure hope we don't get our-selves torpedoed, that's all. Sittin' in one o' them rafts with thirty Krauts and eight enlisted men and a wet ass, that ain't my notion o' the ideal vacation.' Mary Lou began to giggle. Derby said:

'Here's your beer.'

'Sure glad to see it.' Derby took the chit, then stopped and asked Mary Lou:

'A quickie before lunch?'

'You're the boss.'

'Waiter – two more of these, please.' Spatter set his glass down half-empty, and gasped.

'That's cold, all right! Say, where's the Admiral today? Restin' up?'

'Commander Witheringham? I don't know. I suppose he's in his cabin. Our cabin.' Spatter poured the rest of the beer down his throat.

'Guess I'll drop by an' cheer him up. D'ya think he'd appreciate that?' Derby glanced quickly at Mary Lou: she was biting her lips. Derby told Spatter:

'I'm sure he'd love it.'

'Yeah . . . Retirin' sort o' feller, ain't he? Not exactly one o' th' gang. Am I right?'

'I dare say you are.' Derby nodded. 'I'm sure he'd be delighted to see you. Cabin three.'

'Yeah, I'll do that.' Spatter stood up. 'See ya later, folks.' He went out, and the drinks came in on the other swing of the door. When the waiter had gone, Mary Lou said:

'Bill —'

'Yes?'

'Oh – last night. You must think I'm a —'

'No, I don't!'

She laughed at him.

'You don't think I'm a – what?'

'Anything at all. Perhaps you're, well, lonely. That's probably all.'

'Am I being psycho-analysed?'

'Certainly not. You asked what I thought, and I told you.'

'You've given the matter some thought, anyway.' Derby felt the subject could just as well be dropped. He said:

'Cheers.'

'Cheers. But I don't agree with your answer.'

'Do we have to have an answer?'

She smiled at him over the rim of her glass.

'How right you are. We don't, do we?'

Derby put his glass down, suddenly, and stared at the sun-

68

light streaming in through the big, square windows of the lounge. He stood up, and crossed over to look outside. Mary Lou asked:

'What's to look at?' He came back to her.

'We've altered course.'

'Isn't that the zigzag?'

'No – a lot more than that. Oh well. We'd better drink up, I suppose – that lunch gong'll go any minute now.' Her eyes lit up. 'Goody! I've got quite an—' A harsh, staccato buzzing drowned her voice. Loud and insistent, five rings at a time, then a pause and five more: suddenly, outside on deck, shouts and the sound of running feet. Derby shot across the lounge and grabbed Mary Lou by the arm, yanked her up out of the chair.

'That's Emergency. Hurry – fetch your lifebelt and meet me up top!'

'Top?' Slightly fuddled, she didn't get it. She stared at him vacantly and asked: 'What emergency, Bill?' Impatiently, he pushed her out through the swing door.

'Boat Stations. Where we were this morning. Come on, *run*!' The ship heeled over suddenly under sharp rudder, and Mary Lou fell back against him. At the same time the waiter came flying out of his pantry, and crashed into them: Derby pushed him off, and disentangled Mary Lou, who had clutched him round the neck to stop herself falling. Ignoring the waiter, who looked as if he was going to burst into tears, he took Mary Lou by her elbows and propelled her up the slanting deck. Men were running in all directions, and their shouts and whistles blowing made so much noise you could hardly hear the alarm buzzer that was still blasting away, five at a time.

V

All the way, she kept asking him what it was about, why did they have to do this when they'd done it already this morning? He told her: Because this time it's real, it's an Emergency, and she asked him how could he tell? — they hadn't been torpedoed or anything, there'd been no explosion, had there? She said: It must be just another practice, and damn it, she was hungry, it was plain silly to do this right at a meal time. All the way along there were sailors pushing past them and that infernal din: what with that and her questions, he was glad when they reached the door of her cabin. He pushed her in.

'Now. Where's your lifebelt?'

'I don't know. Really, I haven't the faintest —'

'You had it this morning. And you left it here on your way down to the —'m. Here it is.' He'd found it lying in a corner hidden by the lid of an open suitcase. He pushed it over her head and tied the straps around her waist, doubled round and the knot in front, over her tummy: then he pulled out the rubber inflation pipe and blew the thing up. It took a lot of his breath and he didn't waste any more on an answer when she looked at him crossly and said:

'Really, Bill, this is *silly*! You look as if you were having a feed!' He thought: It's my fault, I shouldn't have given her so many John Collinses. He opened the door and pulled her out of the cabin. Withers was standing just outside, blowing up his own Mae West. He looked at them both and his eyes widened.

'*Derby!* What were you – in —?'

'Take Mary Lou up to the boat, there's a good chap. I'm going to get my lifebelt. See you up there.' Withers said:

'Spatter took it. He just snatched it and rushed out before I could stop him.' Withers pointed at the open door of Mary Lou's cabin: inside, pink underclothes were hanging up to dry on strings that she'd strung across. 'I must say, Derby, I'm *extremely* surprised to find —'

'Oh, shut up.' Derby pulled Mary Lou along behind him, up to the boat-deck, and Withers trailed along still struggling with the tapes of his lifebelt.

As soon as they reached it, Derby realized that the boat-deck was where most of the noise was coming from. It was a shambles of shouting Norwegians. A few of them were working around the boats, casting loose the lanyards that secured their canvas covers, overhauling the rope falls, even turning them out on the crane-like davits, but the majority of the men were simply milling about and shouting at each other. The waiter was standing all by himself, crying. As Derby watched, a small grey-templed man in a suit of white overalls and a gold-peaked cap burrowed out of the crowd and, hurrying with short quick strides to the waiter, dealt him a powerful blow in the face. The waiter stopped crying then, and stood stiffly with his arms straight down at his sides as if he expected to be shot now and would like to have it done quickly. He didn't look at the little man who'd hit him, he just stood there like a tall, pale weed in the centre of an open space, and the little man seemed satisfied with that. He rushed back to the boat and began to scream what sounded like abuse at the sailors who were turning it out: but they took no notice of him at all, so he gave that up and darted across to where Derby and the other two were waiting.

'You passengers? You?' Derby looked down at him.

'Yes. Who the hell are you?'

'You in my boat, you passengers! Fall in, please!' Withers bristled at this curt order.

'What the devil d'you mean, *Fall in*? Go and get —'

'Stuffed.' Derby said it for him. 'When the boat's turned out, and the Captain orders us to abandon ship, we'll get in it. For the time being, please mind your own damn business.' Mary Lou got her word in, too.

'You *nasty* little man! Why did you hit that poor boy? I think you're *horrid*.' Withers muttered:

'I think he must be the Chief Engineer.'

71

'*Yais!*' The man pointed at his own chest, and bounced up and down. 'Chief Engineer! Fall in, pliss, qvick!' Derby told him:

'Go away, will you.' He said to Withers: 'I suppose I ought to go and find a lifebelt.' Withers nodded.

'Spatter took yours. I couldn't stop him.' The Second Officer, Eriksen, came through the crowd, peering to right and left. When he saw the passengers, he came up and saluted.

'Captain Christiansen sending compliment, ond vish inform is no dangers, no causings to alarms. Look-out man is reporting periscope, bot mos' likely vos only —' The torpedo struck *Gangerolf* right up for'ard, just under her stern on the starboard side. The explosion was vast, a shattering roar and a tall sheet of flame and water and flying metal over the bow, a sudden reek of scorching paint: the shock of it and the blast sent them headlong, bouncing and rolling on the deck, and the ship reared up and then swung down, listing to starboard and swinging sluggishly as she lost way, down by the head within seconds of the impact. Derby rose shakily to his feet, and helped Mary Lou up. Withers didn't bother, he just sat where he'd fallen, astonishment and fright all over his face. The Second Officer said:

'Vos periscope, all right.' He left them, and ran for'ard. Derby said:

'Don't worry, Mary Lou. I'll look after you. Come on, Withers, get up!' All over the deck, men were struggling to their feet and hurrying to the boats: they were quiet now, probably because they realized for the first time that this was real and not just a more elaborate version of the morning drill. The boats swung out, and some of them were already on their way down to the water. The Second Officer came tearing aft again, shouting something in Norwegian, or Danish perhaps, and he yelled it at the passengers too. Seeing their lack of understanding, he smiled and told them in English:

'Abondon sheep. Very sorry.' Derby said:

'That's all right, old man. Not your fault.' He turned to the others. 'Let's get in that boat.' They went over, and the Chief Engineer told them, quite levelly:

'Yomp in, pliss.' Derby nodded.

'Thanks, we will. Up with you, Mary Lou.' He helped her up the net and she scrambled into the boat. Withers and Derby followed her and behind them came a straggle of Scandinavians, all very silent and no signs at all of that earlier panic. Mary Lou said:

'They *might* have served lunch first.' One of the sailors, who understood English, laughed and translated her remark to his friends. They all bellowed with mirth and looked her over as if they hadn't seen her before. She didn't seem to realize it was anything she'd said, just straightened herself on the thwart and pulled her skirt down over her knees. Derby sat down and put his arm round her. She murmured:

'Well, this *is* cosy.' Withers, on the opposite thwart, objected.

'I hardly think, especially in public and at a time like this, Derby, that —'

'Shut up, Withers.' The boat was just about full, now, and the hands on deck were starting to lower away, but more men were still crowding in. The Chief Engineer, still on deck, tried to divert them, pointing at other boats, but apparently the ones these men had been detailed for had already been lowered without them and they didn't like the idea of getting wet. So they ignored the little Engineer, and scrambled in. Derby said quietly to Withers:

'This craft is overloaded by about two hundred per cent.' Withers, on his dignity now, looked away as if he hadn't heard. Derby pointed at him, and told Mary Lou:

'You know, honey, that man there is one of the silliest creatures God ever saved from a watery death.' She nodded, with her cheek against his shoulder.

'But He hasn't saved him, yet.' Withers glanced at her sharply, and Derby thought: I'm really behaving very badly. The boat was going down, and as they passed deck-level he saw that *Gangerolf* now had a considerable list to starboard. He thought: She won't last long, and he realized that the boat would be just about scraping her side before they touched the sea. He was thinking about that when the submarine's first

73

shell hit: it burst on the boat-deck and killed the men who were manning the boat's falls. The boat went down stern first with a run and then one of the falls jammed in the sheave and snapped. The boat's stern dropped while the bow fall still held part of the weight, and in the wild, detached knowledge of unavoidable disaster Derby thought: That submarine must be Japanese, it can't be German. No civilized race would bombard a sinking ship before her boats were in the water. As he thought it he was somersaulting backwards out of the falling boat, and while he was upsidedown in space, still holding Mary Lou, somebody's boot kicked out all his front teeth. He was still turning over and over as he fell, and the falling seemed to take five minutes while the ship's side and the lifeboat's bottom revolved and vanished: he was looking down at the sea and then it was the riveted plates in *Gangerolf*'s side again and then the boat coming down after him: he'd lost Mary Lou and he was swallowing blood. He hit the sea flat on his back and it jarred right through him but still he went on down into it, and down until he was thinking: I'll *have* to come up soon, this is silly, but he was still going down and his lungs hurt. Suddenly he knew that he was travelling upwards, and he opened his eyes to look but it took so long that he began to think he'd stopped and was just floating under the surface in an unusual state of neutral buoyancy. But it got lighter and he was looking for the surface when his head hit something hard and solid, and when he came to, only a few seconds later probably, he was breathing air but it was pitch dark. He trod water, thinking: *I'm blind*, and in something like panic he called out: I can't see, is anyone there? The blood choked him and there was salt water in it as well, he had the impression that he was vomiting but he wasn't sure of that. He grabbed into the dark with one hand, and it met solid wood close by his face: groping upwards, he found it there too, curving like a roof, and at once he realized that he'd surfaced inside a capsized boat. It must have been the edge of it that his head had hit as he'd risen like a cork.

He pulled himself under the submerged gun'l of the boat, and a moment later he was blinking at the daylight, the blinding sun. He was only a couple of feet from the ship's side, between it and the boat. The ship was listing violently to starboard, away from him, and he thought instinctively: I must get away from her. Then he remembered Mary Lou and started looking round for her: he could hear the submarine's shells exploding on the ship and he felt glad to be on this side, away from that.

Mary Lou was clinging to the boat's rudder, on the other side of it, and when he came splashing and gasping round the stern and she saw him, she made a pleased noise like a cat's mew. He still couldn't speak, only spit mouthfuls of blood, but he was extremely happy to have found her so easily and he stretched out one arm and squeezed her wet shoulder: she was floating easily in her lifebelt. She pointed towards the boat's bow and gasped:

'Withers.' Derby pulled himself around her, to the outboard side, and there, sure enough, was Withers, with his eyes tight shut, groaning, stuck like a limpet to the boat's side. There was nobody else near at all: the other boats were a hundred yards off, and in the space between a number of men were swimming steadily out towards them, away from the ship. Derby thought: Perhaps we could make it. He meant, those other boats. He doubted if he'd manage the distance himself, because he was still dizzy from that crack on the head and his throat was never clear of blood. But for the sake of the others it'd be worth a try. He dragged himself up close to Mary Lou and pointed out at the boats. Still pointing, he looked away from her while he cleared his mouth of blood, then turned back and croaked:

'Swim!' He got the word out fast before the blood came back. She stared at him in a worried sort of way and shook her head.

'Too far. And boats too full, no room.' He knew she was right. He hated this blood he was losing, not just because he was losing it and hating the taste of it but also because he was worried that its smell in the water might attract shark and barracuda. He thought: Well, I dare say there's more blood than just mine. This little contribution won't make much odds,

75

if the fish are coming they'll come. But we'd better get away from the ship.

He hauled himself along the boat and grabbed Withers by his right shoulder. Withers opened his eyes and stared wildly at Derby as he if saw this as an attempt to drown him: to give the man confidence, Derby let go of the shoulder and beckoned. He wanted Withers to come down to the stern, where Mary Lou was. Withers went on shaking his head and glaring at Derby in what was obviously fright. Derby thought: There's nothing else for it: he edged up close, put his arm around Withers's neck with his forearm under the little man's chin, and dragged him aft. Withers gasped and struggled and quite plainly he thought Derby was trying to finish him off. At the boat's stern, Derby let go: Withers grabbed frantically at the stern-post beside Mary Lou, and clung there with his face against the boat's planks. Turning his head, he gaped fearfully at Derby; Derby grinned, trying to convey reassurance, but blood poured down his chin and Withers looked away quickly. Derby hit him on the arm to regain his attention, then worked himself round Mary Lou so that he was dead astern of the boat. He got his hands up on the rudder and began to swim with his legs, pushing the boat forward. Upside down and half sunk, it only just moved, but Mary Lou got the idea at once and joined him, and between them they soon had the boat under way. It began to slide ahead, and Withers, finding himself beside them at the stern, joined in. Derby pointed out to sea, away from the ship, and after a short battle with the unwieldly craft they managed to swing its bow around in that direction. Very slowly, they forged ahead, gradually increasing the distance between themselves and the ship. It was a terribly slow progress, and Derby felt worse at each stroke. Kicking with his legs sent pain shooting through his head, and several times he felt so ill that he had an urge to give up: he wanted to relax, to accept defeat, to lie face downwards in the sea and not even try to breathe. But each time that the idea assumed definite shape in his mind, he found himself vomiting, and the weakness passed with it.

They were about forty yards clear of *Gangerolf* when she

sank. They heard the roar of the sea pouring into her holds, the vast rush of air driven out, and they stopped swimming and watched her go. She went down bow-first, sitting up vertically for a minute or so with her propeller shafts pointing at the sky, then sliding under at first slowly but then, towards the end, in a sudden rush as if she wanted to get if over quickly. When she was gone, a great, smooth ripple a couple of feet high spread out from her dive and rocked them in its passing. At the same time, Derby saw the submarine.

It had been lying stopped about a thousand yards off the ship, on her other side, and it must have been shelling her right up to the last minute, because he could see men still working round her gun. As he watched, she gathered way: he saw the bow-wave rise and spread aft along her tanks as she increased speed. Derby motioned urgently to Mary Lou and Withers to get round on the blind side of the boat, and he himself, with his head only just above water, hung close to the rudder where he could keep an eye on the enemy but run little risk of being seen. He'd heard all about Japanese submarines, and their treatment of survivors.

The Jap was passing close to where *Gangerolf*'s stern had been, five minutes ago, and seemed to be heading for the farthest boats. But suddenly Derby saw the bow-wave shorten and drop, and, looking for some reason for this (it seemed too much to hope that the submarine was about to dive, to leave them in peace) he saw that a little farther out to the North, where the Jap was now stopping, was a cluster of what looked like wreckage. Then he remembered the Carley floats, and he thought: Spatter, and his Germans, and at the same moment a machine-gun started firing from the submarine's bridge. It fired for some time, in short bursts, no doubt shifting its aim from one target to another, and in between the bursts of fire, screams drifted faintly over the water. Derby thought: If it wasn't that you knew, you could easily imagine that sound as coming from a Bank Holiday crowd at Margate. He wasn't shocked, or surprised: this was what they'd always been told they could expect, from the Japanese. It was an animal, a savage, behind that gun, nothing that could be called a man.

Now the firing stopped: one voice was shouting, all alone, and when it stopped a different voice answered it, high-pitched. Men were climbing down from the submarine's bridge on to her casing, and it looked from this distance as if they were taking survivors aboard. There was a crowd around the gun platform, just for'ard of the bridge: it was hard to see what was going on, but after a few minutes there were a lot of men climbing up into the bridge and a small group of about five or six walking slowly for'ard, towards the bow. The casing was clear except for that small group, still walking for'ard, and Derby was watching and wondering what it was all about when the machine-gun opened up again. The men up for'ard went down in a heap, all except one who started running aft towards the bridge with his hands up, but the machine-gun got him before he was halfway there, it was finished with the others so it gave him a burst: he seemed to leap up in the air before he dropped. The gun stopped, and there was something foul even in its silence.

Derby saw the submarine gathering way again, heading in towards the boats. He turned to Mary Lou. Her face was the colour of dirty linen and she looked bewildered, like a child that's lost its parents in a strange town. He grasped her arm, and she stared through him as if he wasn't there, as if neither of them was: as if this wasn't a thing she could believe was true. He turned his face away and spat, then he told her:

'Under the boat. It'll be all right.' He pointed at the water at the edge of the boat, making a diving motion with his hand, and he banged his hand on the side of it and spat again and told her: 'Get under.' Thank God, she understood. She took a breath and pinched her nose between the thumb and forefinger of her left hand, and disappeared under the water. He felt her under water until she was up inside the boat. Then he jerked his head at Withers, telling him to do the same, and Withers, to Derby's intense surprise, just nodded and ducked under. Derby took a quick look over his shoulder: the Jap was going to pass pretty close. He held his breath and pulled himself down under the side of the boat and up underneath it again into the air. It was dark inside. He hooked one arm over a thwart

78

that was just about level with the water, and groped with his free hand for Mary Lou: almost immediately he touched her wet hair, and he stroked her cheek with his fingers: she took hold of his hand, and held it, and they moved their joined hands until they located Withers, and the three of them, holding hands in the dark, waited for the submarine to pass.

Derby wondered what time it was. He was working it out in his mind, thinking that it must have been about twelve-thirty when the alarm went, perhaps one o'clock when the ship was hit: after that, well, it could only be a guess, say, half-past two now? Suddenly he realized that there was still a watch on his wrist, and it was supposed to be watertight, shock-proof, all sorts of things. He held it up close in front of his eyes, but there was no luminosity at all. He put it against his ear, and heard the ticking, and he thought: I should write to the makers about that, they'd be delighted to know. Probably surprised, too. He latched himself on to the thwart again, and began to think about sharks. Hanging there in the dark with all but his head and shoulders in the sea, it wasn't difficult to imagine them nosing round. Once, on patrol in Japanese waters, he'd rescued a bunch of American flyers who'd been shot down on their way back from a bombing mission: one of them, who'd been in the water for some hours because he'd dropped a long way from the rest and had no rubber float to climb into, had been gnawed by barracuda (Derby hadn't realized before that barracuda would just nibble like that, he'd always imagined them biting to kill and being done with it), and when they got him out of the water his lower half wasn't pretty. He'd died a couple of days later, they'd done their best but without a doctor their best was limited: when he died he wasn't feeling any pain, anyway, because they'd filled him up with rum.

There was a tremor in the water and it became a sound that echoed in the small space in which the three of them were breathing. Derby recognized it at once as propeller noise, it was so clear and regular that he could count the revolutions, the throbs, just as if he was listening at the earphones of an Asdic set. It grew louder all the time and Mary Lou asked suddenly, in a whisper that was loud in that confined space:

'Bill, what is it?' He tightened his grip on her hand and told her:

'Submarine, passing close. Don't worry.' He thought: I hope it *will* just pass. It would be typical of those bastards to ram the capsized boat in their destructive joy. The noise of the screws was louder each second and he could feel it in the water as well as hear it. The sound was quite familiar: he'd not only listened to it often enough over an Asdic set (when it was called Hydrophone Effect) but he'd heard it dozens of times during depth-charge attacks when destroyers were passing close overhead. It gave him an unpleasant sensation in his stomach, but this tuned in with the sound to form a known pattern, and the meaning of the pattern was a necessity to appear undisturbed. He told Mary Lou and Withers:

'It's giving us a wide berth.' At the same time he thought: The swine's getting a damn sight too close, he's going to ram us. He thought: Perhaps they saw our heads, before we ducked. The noise of the screws was very much louder now and he would have needed to shout to make the others hear him, so he stayed quiet and suddenly it occurred to him that prayer might help.

He decided against it. If you prayed at all, you prayed regularly, and in all circumstances, not only fear. If you only prayed when your disturbed guts told you to, you might as well save your breath. If you made a habit of prayer, you had a right to resort to it at a time like this: if not, well, you'd as much as turned down the invitation earlier on and there was no reason to believe that you had the right of a rain-check.

The propeller noise ran until it was a roar that filled the upturned boat, and while in himself he was filled with fear and certainty that this was the end of them, he kept himself still and held their hands firmly, thinking: If this is the worst, we've had it anyway, and no amount of objections can change that now: if I'm wrong and the submarine is only passing, any move any of us make will be suicide.

The noise rose to a crescendo and the submarine's bow-wave lifted the boat and threw it sideways. He lost the hands he'd been holding and grabbed for a firmer hold on the thwart as the boat rocked wildly and swung around: then it rose, taking him up with it until he began to think that it was only one side of it that was rising, that it was rolling over into its natural position. But as violently as it had risen, now it fell back: a wave rose inside the boat and he was swallowing water, he thought: *I'll have to get out*, but the wave dropped again and the boat was only rolling gently, still upside down, and he reached out to find Mary Lou: if she hadn't been hanging on hard she could easily have been washed out under the gun'l. He couldn't find her, and he'd let go of the thwart to get himself for'ard and find her when the submarine's wake lifted the boat again and rolled it over almost on its side. He had a glimpse of daylight and of a wave's curling surface and a hand close to his face: he snatched at it and held on and the boat crashed down again and it was dark and quiet and Withers shouted: 'Help!'

Derby yelled, furious but making as much noise himself: 'Blast you, keep quiet!' As he shouted he realized that his mouth wasn't bleeding any more: salt water, he thought. Withers's voice came back quietly out of the dark. He sounded surprised.

'That you, Derby?'

'Who the hell d'you think it is? Mary Lou, are you all right?'

'Yes, Bill. Fine.' Withers said, in a high, frightened voice: 'I thought *this* was you.'

'What d'you mean, *this*?' He had Mary Lou's hand in his, and the boat was steady. The air was fresher, too, thanks to that violent roll that'd let new air in. Withers said:

'There's – someone else here. It's – dead, I think.' All of them heard the machine-gun start. It was closer than it had been last time it fired, and the bursts were longer, possibly because a lifeboat is a bigger target than a Carley float and holds more people. The shouts came again, too, and the high screams, and Mary Lou began to cry. She was obviously trying not to, and once she stopped and said, *I'm sorry*, but she couldn't hold it back for longer than that. She went on crying and Derby pulled her across to his thwart and held her close against him and while she cried he could feel her body shaking as hard as if the bullets from that gun were going into her, all of them, she was taking them all into her own flesh and they were tearing her to shreds and leaving only the sound of her grief in the dozen cubic feet of dark around them. The gun seemed to take a long time to finish its business, but it must have done it thoroughly because when it stopped there was no sound at all, not from the outside. Only inside, Mary Lou's sobbing and the water lapping on the boat's sides. Derby thought: Odd, no fish yet.

VI

There'd been silence for a long time, the gun and the other noises had stopped and then Mary Lou had stopped crying, and the three of them had been hanging there in the dark without a word or a movement. Derby felt sure that the submarine must have left, most likely dived, but all the same he wasn't taking the risk of coming out and being spotted. The trapped air was foul, now, and before long they'd have to do something about it, but for as long as they could breathe at all the discomfort was better than the possible alternative of bullets.

To Derby, a greater worry than the shortage of air was the likelihood of fish arriving. After the machine-gunning, the water'd be full of them, and while for the moment they'd no doubt be fully occupied in the two areas of slaughter, it was reasonable to assume that sooner or later they'd be cruising farther afield: new arrivals, particularly, excited by the smell and finding no ready victums with which to satisfy their hunger.... Derby thought: Perhaps we ought to chance it, and make a move. Suddenly Withers broke the silence.

'I can't breathe! Derby, there's no air! I'm going outside—'

'No.' Derby'd had his mind made up for him. But he didn't like the idea of Withers going out first, perhaps splashing clumsily about and attracting attention, if there was any attention to attract. 'Hang on just a minute, while I take a quick look. Then I'll come back and give you the all clear.'

Withers's voice was plaintive in the dark.

'Why shouldn't *I*? I tell you I can't stand—'

'Please. Look after Mary Lou, will you? Withers?'

'Well, all right. But hurry.'

'Good man. Are you all right, Mary Lou?'

'I'm fine, Bill.' She didn't sound fine. Withers asked, in a high voice:

'Derby, are you going or not? Otherwise I'll —'

'I'm off.' Derby took a breath and pulled himself under the surface, close to the side of the boat: he felt the gun'l scrape over the top of his head and he held on tight so as to be sure of coming up slowly and making no disturbance in the water.

The light was blinding, and for a minute he couldn't keep his eyes open. But the air was good! When his eyes had adjusted themselves to the glare, he looked around him.

The sea was dead flat, as smooth and shiny as oiled glass. It looked as if you'd be able to skate on it. Derby saw that he was just about in the centre of a wide circle of wreckage: planks, pieces of boats, broken rafts, tins. Within a yard of him a body floated face downwards, hanging in its lifebelt. There were a lot more of them, farther away. There wasn't a breath of wind: the submarine's wash must have churned up all this flotsam and sent it drifting in different directions.

He hauled himself round to the other side of the lifeboat: no submarine on this side, either. The Japanese had gone, leaving only the rubbish, the wreckage, and the bodies. There was a hard knot in the lower part of his stomach, and he thought: I'll always remember this, any time in the years to come that I see a Japanese and am led into mistaking him for a man, I'll remember this and — He pulled himself together. He was shaking with rage and he'd been talking aloud to himself. He thought, staring at a body that was floating on its back a dozen yards away: We'll need all the strength we have just to stay alive. Mustn't waste it getting angry. Suddenly he saw the water swirl, around that corpse: he watched it almost unbelievingly and it began to move, glided about a yard and a half and then vanished, down into the sea. Derby was mesmerized by that patch of water, he stared at it, somehow fascinated and at the same time shocked into inertia. Then, to his own great surprise, he was violently sick, and the fit passed.

He'd hardly surfaced inside the boat (it stank, now that he'd been outside) when Withers asked:

'That you, Derby? Is it all right? Can we get out?'

'Yes. And get on top of the boat. Go now, Withers, and

84

hurry.' He found Mary Lou's hand, and gripped it. 'Come on, Mary Lou. With me. Ready?' They went under together, and when they were outside he hung on to the boat with one hand and began to push her up with the other. She blinked at him, and floundered.

'Wait, Bill. I can't see.'

'Not necessary. Get up there, *please*.' The boat was rocking under Withers's efforts to mount it, from the other side, and now he appeared on top. Derby grabbed his foot.

'Here, Withers. Pull her up. I'll push.' Between them they got her up out of the water, and then Derby climbed up over the stern-post. She told him:

'I still can't see.' She was rubbing her eyes. Derby said, quietly:

'Listen, Mary Lou. When you *can*, when you *can* see, don't look too hard. There's a lot of – well, bodies, and —'

'I know, Bill. I've been thinking about them. Won't cry again, I promise I won't ... Bill, what do we do now? Wait to be rescued?'

He laughed. Not that there was anything to laugh at.

'First thing is to get our breath back. Then we'll have to get ourselves over to one of those other boats, before this one sinks. It can't last for ever.' Two boats were afloat, the right way up, some way off on the edge of the circle. He studied them closely, and saw that one was very low in the water, probably holed. The other looked undamaged. He pointed at it, and told her: 'That one.'

Withers stared at it, and nodded.

'A long way. I suppose we'll have to swim.'

'No.' Derby shook his head. 'We won't swim.' Mary Lou was still rubbing her eyes: there was mascara all over her face in streaks, and most probably it was blinding her too. Derby told Withers: 'We won't swim, old man,' and he pointed at a floating corpse that was jerking up and down in the water as if it was being tugged at from below. Well, it *was*. Withers shouted:

'My God! Shark!'

'No, old man. That's barracuda. But there's shark here too.'

Withers looked frightened to death. He stammered:

'We've been down there all this time and there've been—'

'Seems so. But we're up *here*, now, so we may as well relax.'
Mary Lou took him literally: she lay face downwards along
the keel, straddling it with her arms and legs. She had her eyes
shut and he said: 'That's my girl. Take it easy.'

'I don't want to see. Bill, how can we get over there without
swimming?'

'Paddle this thing over, of course.'

'What, with our hands?'

'Only a little way. Just to those planks and stuff. Then we
can pick some up and use them as paddles. It's a piece of cake.
Ready, Withers?'

'I suppose so ... Derby: there's a dead man in the boat. He
was jammed under the thwart.'

'You mentioned it before. Let's get cracking, eh?'

'I took hold of his hand by mistake, Derby, I thought it was
yours, you see, and then when you spoke from the other end of
the boat I—'

'Withers.'

'Yes? I was—'

'Shut up, there's a good chap.' He began to paddle with his
hands, hanging face down over the boat's stern and sweeping
his arms to and fro in the water. Withers did the same thing
over the bow, and the boat crept sluggishly forward at a rate of
about a yard in every five minutes. Mary Lou tried to help,
but from her position amidships she could only reach the water
on one side, hanging on to the keel with her other hand, and
her shifted weight so upset the boat's balance that Derby asked
her to stop. All the time she kept her eyes on the boat's planks,
under her face, because she didn't want to look anywhere else,
and since Derby was facing aft Withers was the only one of
them who knew what progress they were making. After what
must have been three-quarters of an hour, Derby stopped paddling. His arms didn't feel as if they belonged to him, and his
back and the back of his neck were burning with strain.

'Withers. How far?' Withers stopped, too, and twisted
around to answer.

'Only a few yards. Useful-looking timber just ahead.'

'Thank God for that. I feel like the Worry-Worry bird.' Mary Lou asked him:

'What on earth's that?'

'An Australian fowl. Certainly not English. It flies backwards because it doesn't give a damn where it's going but's always terribly anxious to know where it's been.'

She sat up on the boat's spine and stared at the cloudless sky. 'Silly sort of bird. I want to know where we're going. Where *are* we going, Bill?'

'To that lovely watertight boat, Wren Smith.'

'I know that, stupid. But after we get to it?'

He thought: Oh, Mary Lou, I'd have thought better of you than asking such a silly question. He told her:

'One thing at a time. First thing's to get somewhere we can rest, and – damn it, stay alive! After that – think again. Any better ideas?'

'Yes,' she said. 'Paddle. I'm – uncomfortable.'

Derby laughed. It was the best laugh he'd had in half a day.

'Withers. The lady's in discomfort. We'd better steam.' They lowered themselves to the task and began to paddle: Mary Lou laid herself on her back along the ridge of the keel and went on staring at the sky, which was so much easier to look at than the sea. She said, addressing that clean, uncluttered sky:

'It's a lovely day for it.' Nobody answered, they hadn't the breath to spare. 'I mean, if it'd been rough, really quite rough, it would have been much more difficult, wouldn't it?'

Derby grunted, missing a stroke as he spoke over his shoulder.

'Much worse. We'd be dead.' He was silent for a minute or two, paddling with his heavy, nerveless arms. Then he added: 'And by now my back wouldn't be hurting like this. And you wouldn't be uncomfortable.' She told him:

'I'm not uncomfortable, I'm *sore*.'

Withers had stopped paddling.

'Derby – here it is!' He was pulling a sort of grating out of the sea. Derby pushed himself up and swivelled round to look. It was the midships frame of a sea-boat's bottom boards.

'If we break that up, Withers, the separate parts'll make splendid paddles. One each and a few to spare.' Withers nodded.

'Of course. Why d'you think I picked it up? Been steering at it for hours.'

'Well done, old man.' Way over in the West, the sun was on its way down. 'Let's take it to bits. Be as well to get over there before dark, eh?'

He looked wearily at the frame of thick boards: 'Wish we had a screwdriver.'

'Have to break it.'

Derby edged around Mary Lou. Her cotton dress was dry and stiff with salt, now, not clinging to her as it had been an hour ago. Her hair hung straight down all round her head, and her face was still streaked with mascara. Seeing him look at her, she flushed and put a hand to her hair.

'I must be quite an eyeful.'

'Rather attractive, as a matter of fact ... Thanks.' He took one end of the frame from Withers, and they crashed it against the boat's keel until it was cracked and broken in several places and both of them had splinters in their hands. Then they pulled the thing apart and took a couple of planks each, and Derby climbed back to the stern.

Withers started paddling over the port bow, so Derby put his plank down over the quarter on the starboard side, and they soon had the boat moving. It was harder work than the old way, but it pushed the boat along much faster. In about twenty minutes, they were closing up to the other boat. As they approached it, Derby saw that the inside of it was about as bad as he'd expected, if not worse. He stopped paddling, and told Mary Lou:

'You in the middle there. Promise me something, please.' She smiled at him.

'For you, honey, *anything*.'

'Keep looking out that way. Don't under any circumstances look at the boat we're heading for until we've – got it fixed up.' She wasn't smiling now.

'All right, Bill. I promise.' He called to Withers:

'Better come up astern of it and slide alongside, don't you think?' Withers didn't answer, he just went on paddling with his eyes fixed on that other boat. Another minute, and they rested, and the boat carried on, losing way until it had almost stopped by the time it bumped against the other's quarter. Withers looked back at Derby, over his shoulder: his face was as white as a sheet.

'Derby. I don't think I can —'

'You hold on. Just keep us alongside.' He climbed round Mary Lou again, she was sitting stiffly, staring out to sea, and as he passed she shifted to let him by without looking at his face. He got himself past her and close up behind Withers. Withers was holding on to the keel with his right hand and the gun'l of the other boat with his left: he had his eyes shut and his lips were moving as if he was praying. Perhaps he was.

There was a small space right in the sten-sheets of that other boat. Derby climbed down, very slowly and cautiously because the thought of stumbling and falling into the middle of that boat was worse than any nightmare.

Presently he was there. Hanging over the stern beside him was a sailor with no top to his head: it had been shot off. Derby began to tip him up so that he'd slide over the side: it looked from the position he was in, that he'd been trying to get over when the machine-gun stopped him. Derby was heaving him over when he noticed that the man wore a seaman's knife, British Admiralty pattern, on a lanyard round his waist. Derby opened the knife and cut the lanyard: robbing the dead was one thing, staying alive was another, and a knife could be terribly useful later on. In fact, it was useful know: before he let the body go over the side, he slashed its lifebelt open so that it'd sink. Then he turned to the next one, a young man in overalls with his mouth open as if he was shouting. He'd been shot in the chest, neck and head. Quite clearly, the Japanese had given this boat their most careful attention, there'd been nothing haphazard in their shooting. Nothing half-hearted. Derby ripped a hole in another lifebelt, and dragged its owner to the side. There were eleven of them, altogether, and by the time the job was half done he was exhausted. After the last few hours, it was pretty amazing that he could lift a feather.

He turned the next body over, to get a grip on its shoulders; the head rolled over, and flopped, and Derby jerked back as if something heavy had hit him between the eyes: that was how it felt. The man he'd turned over was Captain Christiansen. Part of his jaw was gone. Derby's mind reeled, at first in rage, a maniacal hate that screamed for a Jap to tear apart in savage retribution, then, suddenly, as he looked down at the Captain's closed eyes, in overwhelming sorrow. He told himself: After this war, I'll find those boys of his, in Norway. He bent down, put his arms around the shoulders of the man he'd drunk whisky with forty-eight hours ago, dragged him to the side and rolled him over into the sea. As the body sank into the quiet water Derby began to murmur what he could remember of the Naval funeral prayer, but the words wouldn't come, only an awful pain as though he'd lost his own brother, flesh and blood, his own, and suddenly he was crying, he couldn't stop it, he was crying noisily like a woman. Withers looked up, and stared. Mary Lou heard too: she turned and saw Derby with tears pouring down his face and without any hesitation she scrambled for'ard and climbed down to join him. She didn't say anything, she just helped him finish, and Withers climbed down too. He let the other boat go.

When the last body was over the side, Mary Lou put her arms round Derby as if he was a child. He didn't see or feel her, he stood there while she held him with her head pressed against his chest and crooned like a mother to her baby.

'Don't, oh please, you mustn't —' Suddenly he noticed her. He took her by the shoulders and gently prised her off him. He told her, hoarsely:

'You promised me you'd —'

'I know, Bill. I'm sorry.'

They looked round at the boat. It was scarred and holed, but fortunately there were no holes anywhere near the waterline. None that they could see. But it was in a terrible mess. Derby looked about for something to clean up with, but there wasn't anything, so he pulled his shirt off, wet it over the side, and began to use it as a swab. His mind was dead, drained of emotion. When the shirt was heavy with blood, he wrung it out over the side and started again.

'Give me that.' Mary Lou snatched it out of his hands, and went to work on her knees. He stood limply in the stern-sheets, exhausted in mind and body, but somehow not wanting to sit down even after the thwarts had been washed clean. Suddenly Withers shouted:

'Thank God! It's full!'

'Eh?' Derby looked down at him. He was squatting, close to Derby's feet, holding a small barrico that he'd unlashed from under the stern seat. There was another, under the seat on the other side. Withers said triumphantly:

'Water! This one's full!' He was rocking it in his hands, against his ear. Mary Lou asked:

'Can we have a drink, Bill?' She glanced down at Withers and back again. 'Just a little? I'm terribly thirsty.' Withers stood up, holding the cask under his arm. He said:

'Look. *I* am the senior officer. *I'm* in charge.' He stood there looking at Derby as if he expected his authority to be challenged. Derby nodded, wearily.

'Of course. You're in charge. Let's have a drink.'

'Very well. A small drink each. Then no more until the morning. It may be some days before we're picked up.' Mary Lou snorted angrily:

'You've been reading books. Hurry up, I'm thirsty.' Withers chose not to hear her. He gazed helplessly up at Derby.

'How can we get the bung out?' Derby pulled the seaman's knife out of the pocket of his shorts, and opened the spike on it.

'Here.' Without looking down, he handed it to Withers.

'Splendid!' Withers bent over the cask. 'Where'd you get this, Derby? I never saw you carrying one, before.' Derby told him:

'I found it.' Mary Lou came aft.

'Why don't you rest, Bill?'

'Uh? Oh, rest. Yes, I will.' She put her hand on his arm.

'The first step, usually, is to sit down.' He stared down at the thwart, it glistened wet and yellowish in the dying sun, and she said: 'It's quite clean, now. I've washed it.' Withers stood up, holding the barrico in his arms as if it was a baby.

'You first.' He held it out to Mary Lou.

'How on earth can I drink out of *that*?' Withers snapped, impatiently:

'Put your mouth to the bung hole, and I'll tip it. Just a couple of swallows, mind.'

When she'd drunk, and most of her two swallows had run down over her chin, he offered it to Derby, who took it in his two hands and drank quickly as though he'd been drinking out of barrels all his life. Then Withers took his turn, and banged the bung in again with the palm of his hand.

Derby lowered himself to the bottom boards, and stretched out flat with his legs under the thwart. He closed his eyes, and began to feel drowsy. Then he opened them again, and asked:

'You all right, Mary Lou?'

'I'm fine, Bill. Go to sleep.' Her voice sounded close, and turning his head he found that she was lying beside him, her face not six inches from his. He shifted his hand until it found hers. In a minute, he was asleep.

When he awoke, it was blowing half a gale. The boat was swinging violently, pitching and yawing in a stiff sea: it was its motion that had woken him. He thought at first that he was in his cabin, in the *Gangerolf*, and that someone had opened the deadlight and the scuttle so that the wind was blowing in, and spray too: he was freezing cold. But he felt the hardness of the boards under him, and remembered that he'd gone to sleep in a lifeboat: even from that point he had to rack his brains for the rest of it. The details came slowly into his mind, and turning his head, he found Mary Lou still fast asleep beside him: her head and body were moving from side to side as the boat rocked and pitched and slanted across the sea. He sat up, with his eyes at the level of the gun'ls, and watched the curled white tops of waves racing past the boat: on the starboard side, a great dark pile of sea rose and towered and broke, spattering over into the boat. From the bow, Wither's voice came anxiously out of the dark.

'Derby? You awake? That you, Derby?' Derby thought: Oh Lord: Withers! Of all people to share *this* with. He called out:

'Yes. How long's this been going on?' Withers came aft, climbing over the thwarts and staggering against the motion of the boat.

'About an hour, I suppose. It's getting worse. Funny thing is, Derby, it started so suddenly. One minute flat calm, then a gust of wind – and now this.' Derby thought: Did you expect to get a postcard first? He stood up, and stared out at the blur of wild water.

'We'd better do something, before it gets really bad.' A big wave burst against the stern, showering them with spray. Derby shouted: 'We'd better rig some sort of sea anchor, Withers, keep her head to the sea.'

'We can't!' Withers was yelling into his ear. 'There's nothing we can use – absolutely nothing! I thought about it, and looked for something.' Derby pointed at a heap of some gear up in the bows.

'What's that?'

'Anchor and a hemp cable. There's nothing else in the boat. We'll just have to hope for the best, Derby.' Derby thought of Saint Paul: when he was in trouble of this sort, he cast four anchors out of the stern and prayed for the day. Fat lot of use that'd be, here. Withers asked: 'Where's Mary Lou?'

'Asleep.'

'We'd better wake her up.'

'What for? Let the girl sleep.' The sea came up and took the boat and drove it forward, up a steep incline of piled water: at the summit the boat paused, slowly toppling forward, then rushed down into the trough. A wave broke under her quarter, slewing her round, and a second wave, much bigger than the others, flung its weight against her side and broke green over her gun'l. Withers grasped Derby by the elbow:

'It's getting worse every minute!'

'Yes.' He sat down on a thwart, and held on tight as the boat slewed right round again and climbed the next wave sideways. To be frank, things were looking extremely nasty. He asked Withers: 'I suppose there's nothing to bale with?'

'Not a thing.' The boat slid sideways over the crest, heeling over until her port gun'l was just about under water: then, slowly righting herself, she whirled round like a top and practically stood up on her bow. Withers staggered, lost his grip and fell forward, clearing the nearest thwart completely and winding himself on the next. Derby climbed over and helped him up. Wind and sea were rising fast. Withers told Derby:

'There's one good thing. I found a tin of biscuits, behind the other barrico.'

'A tin of —? Damn it all, you just said there wasn't anything we could bale with! What's wrong with that?'

'It's a sealed tin, Derby, full of *biscuits*! It's the only food we've got!' Derby thought: Oh no! How stupid can a little man get? He flung himself over to the port side of the boat to balance a savage list the other way: when the danger had passed, he came back amidships and yelled at Withers:

'What'd three corpses do with a lot of biscuits?' As he shouted, the top of a wave drenched him and the bulk of it dropped green into the stern-sheets. 'See what I mean? Where's that tin?'

Withers pointed aft: he looked frightened now, even in the dark Derby could see the stiffness in him. The boat rolled again, wildly, and Withers got right down and wrapped his arms around a thwart: Derby leant his weight on the high side until the boat swung back. He thought: We'll be damn lucky if we come out of this alive. He clambered aft, keeping a wary eye on the sea, then knelt down and groped for the tin. It was there, all right, jammed in behind the barrico, and he dragged it out. A full-size tin of Pusser's biscuits: he thought: Good old Pusser. Then he saw Mary Lou: she'd rolled over to the boat's side, and she was all curled up there, in an inch of water that swilled across the boards. She was still asleep. He bent down, steadying himself with one hand on the gun'l, and shook her by the shoulder until she rolled over and looked up at him.

'Time you woke up, Mary Lou. Sea's a bit rough. You're a ruddy marvel, sleeping through —' He forgot her, hurled himself over to the other side as the boat swung down on its beam ends, shipping foam. For a moment he thought that this was the one she wouldn't come out of, she hung there with the sea trickling over and there didn't seem to be any life in her: but the moment passed and she righted herself. Mary Lou was sitting up.

'It *is* rough. Is it dangerous?'

'Yes.' There wasn't any point in telling her anything else, particularly when Withers was practically gibbering with fear. 'But we'll survive. Come along this way, honey.' He took her hand and helped her up: she was shivering with cold. 'This way.' He guided her for'ard, holding the biscuits under his other arm.

'Withers. Look after Mary Lou. And give me my knife.' Withers passed it over, and took Mary Lou's arm. Derby told her: 'Hold on to something.' He meant, something other than Withers. He squatted down between the thwarts, and stabbed the blade of the knife into the middle of the tin. He levered the blade to and fro like a tin-opener, gradually slitting the tin around its middle so that the two halves would make two balers. It took a long time, and more than once he had to drop the thing and lean over one side or the other to counter the boat's lists with his weight. But at the same time it occurred to him that the lists were less violent: he told himself, sawing at the tin: Nonsense! It seemed ridiculous that the storm's force should have passed so quickly. But for all that, by the time he'd opened three of the tin's sides there was no doubt that the wind was dropping. Biscuits were spilling out into the bottom of the boat: he forced the tin partly open, scooped some out and gave a handful each to Mary Lou and Withers. Then he cut through the fourth side.

'Thing is, what can I do with all these biscuits.' Mary Lou suggested, with her mouth full:

'There's room down in front of my shirt.'

'You're a genius, Mary Lou.' He tipped as many biscuits as he could down her front, while she held the shirt open at its top. Then he filled his own pockets, and Withers did the same, and he went for'ard and poured what was left into the hollow circle of the coiled anchor cable. 'Mary Lou: you go back aft, so we can take up these boards and bale.' She said:

'It's better, isn't it?'

'Definitely. Let's hope it stays better. Off you go.' She climbed aft, and he handed Withers one of the halves of the tin. 'Mind the edges – they're like razors. Let's get the boards up.'

VII

Derby told Withers: 'Careful of that tin's edges. Sharp as hell.' They were squatting, ankle-deep in water, baling. Although the wind had dropped considerably, so that the danger of foundering had passed, it was still blowing strongly enough to send an occasional wave-top slopping into the boat, and they had their work cut out to remove more water than was arriving. Withers had difficulty holding his tin.

'Not a very good baler, Derby.'

'Better than none.' But Withers wanted to grumble.

'I'd have thought we'd had about enough exertion for one day. I'm just about whacked.'

Derby grunted, emptied a canful over the side, and told him:

'You shouldn't have joined, old man.' He could see clearly enough that Withers wasn't trying to do his share of the work: at each dip he only got about a couple of inches of water into his tin, and he took one dip to every two of Derby's. Presently he stopped altogether.

'We aren't making much impression on it, Derby. I don't see there's much point, really —' He rose, groaning, and sat on the edge of the thwart, holding the can in his hands. Derby felt an unusual anger growing inside him.

'We're damn lucky to be alive at all, Withers. If we'd sat around today and said there wasn't any point, we'd be – with the rest of them.'

Withers shrugged. 'Perhaps. But – well, what's the odds? At least they've got it over. We —'

'Withers!' Derby's muscles were tensed hard, he had a job to control himself enough to speak quietly so that Mary Lou wouldn't hear. 'If you say another word of that sort, I'll break your bloody neck and put you over the side. I mean it, Withers. Pull your weight, what there is of it, and shut up. Otherwise, so help me, I swear I'll —'

'Derby! Are you out of your mind? I think you're forgetting that I —'

'That you're the senior officer. In charge. All right, but try to behave like it. Like some sort of man, anyway. If you can do that, I'll call you sir: if you can't – bale, damn you!'

Withers came down off the thwart, and dipped his can in the water.

'I was only having a breather, Derby. As to your abuse, your – threats – it's insubordination. I won't forget it, Derby. You'd better watch your step! If we're picked up, and —'

'Shut up. Just shut up, and bale, will you?'

'Derby, if you think —'

'Yes, I do. Often. And if you utter one word of that defeatist rubbish in front of Mary Lou, I'll put you over my knee and beat your scraggy little bottom, right in front of her.'

'Derby! I'm – I —'

'Look, Withers. Put your tin in the deepest part, here, amidships. Not on the edge where it's shallow. And do it twice as fast, to make up for that – breather, you had.'

They worked in silence, after that, for half an hour of so. Then Derby thought, cooling off: This hasn't improved the situation at all. I should have let him drip, and not worried: certainly I shouldn't have lost my temper.

It surprised him that he had. Normally he wasn't easily moved to anger, he could ignore the small irritations of life and overlook many of those things which drove most men to heat and violence. He thought: I suppose I'm *on edge*. That was the phrase. There was a word, too – what was it? *Overwrought*. That's it, he thought, that's what I am. Now well on the track, he got hold of an even better one: *I'm not myself!* The stupidity of the expression made him laugh aloud.

'What are you laughing at?'

Derby looked up. Withers's face wasn't more than six inches from his own. The pop-eyes stared into his, and the expression was one of rigid preparedness for new insults.

'I'm sorry, Withers. I was just thinking about our recent –

98

exchange. It's so damn silly. We're all – *on edge.* I'm sorry old man.'

Withers looked immensely relieved. He said:

'I accept your apology. Under the circumstances, I'll attribute it to strain, and – er – I'll forget it, Derby.'

'Let's both do that.' Derby dipped his can, it scraped the boards close to the keelson but he could only get an inch of water into it. 'Look, old man. I reckon we've just about cleaned this up. What d'you say? Shall we join the lady?'

She was asleep, but Withers trod on her leg and she woke up. Sat up, too. Withers seeped apologies.

'I'm terribly sorry. Really I'm frightfully —'

'Don't give it another thought, please.' She seemed not only wide awake, but in excellent form. 'Anybody want a biscuit?'

Derby saw what was coming. He had some biscuits in the pockets of his shorts, in fact they were bulging with them, but he wanted to see this.

'I would indeed. Got one handy?'

She delved enthusiastically into the front of her shirt, and began to wriggle. After a moment, while Derby watched the movements of her hand under her shirt and Withers stared out at roughly where in daylight one might expect to find an horizon, she brought out a biscuit.

'Here you are, Bill. It's still warm.' He took it from her without smiling.

'Just the way I always liked them.' He bit into it, and smacked his lips. 'Delectable!' She giggled, and asked Withers:

'One for you?'

He coughed before he told her: 'No, thanks awfully. I – er – I have some, here.' He took one out of his pocket and held it up so she could see it. 'Thanks all the same.'

'Oh, you're mean! I want to get rid of *these*!' She tapped herself on the chest. Derby said quickly:

'Please don't do that.'

'I meant the biscuits, silly. Just as I was dropping off to

sleep I turned over on my tummy and it was *most* uncomfortable. Have another?'

'Keep it warm for me, honey. I'm still revelling in this one.' He munched happily, and told Withers: 'This is the only way to serve ship's biscuits, old man. Soon as we get back, I'll have it put in the Seamanship Manual. Then I'll be famous.' He held out his hand for another, and Mary Lou plunged her hand down her front. It really was worth watching. 'One way to achieve flag rank quickly, Withers, is to have your less interesting thoughts published in the Seamanship Manual.'

Withers changed the subject.

'This wind's from the north-east, Derby, I'd say.'

'East, surely.' He hadn't given the matter a thought. Withers coughed.

'North-east, Derby.'

'Well, let's split the difference, and call it east by north.'

'Very well. Now – I should say it's been blowing for four hours, and an hour or more of that at something near gale force. We must be – some way from where we started.'

Derby had his mouth full. He nodded.

'S' fair assumption.' Withers stared at him, coldly.

'Well, where does that put us?'

'Huh?' Derby sat himself down beside Mary Lou, and studied the pattern of teeth in the biscuit. Mary Lou leant forward, resting her arm on his knee.

'Where *does* it put us, Bill?'

'Rather depends where we started from, I'd say. Give me another biscuit, please.' He had a really close view, this time. He told her: 'You know, I think I could live on these things for weeks.' He took a handful out of his pocket, and put them in her hand. 'Stick 'em in the warmer, there's a dear.'

Withers was facing squarely out to sea.

'Derby. Have you *no* idea where we were when we were sunk?'

'Absolutely none, old man. Have you?'

'No. I have not. But you spent a great deal of time with Captain Christiansen. I thought you'd have —'

'I was drinking his whisky, old man, not picking his brains.

Tell you the truth, I didn't even want to know. I was rather enjoying the feeling of being a passenger. Other blokes doing the chores, you know.'

Mary Lou yawned. 'It must have been a lovely change for you, Bill. What a shame this had to happen and spoil it. . . . Commander Witheringham, can't I *really* press you to a biscuit?'

'I – I have some, thank you. Derby: from what I would have assumed our course to be – an approximation, of course – I should imagine that this drift will have taken us even farther from any normal convoy route, and – er – away from any area of present Naval operations. Would you agree?'

Derby couldn't answer: he had his mouth full again. Mary Lou asked Withers:

'What about land? Islands, or something?'

Withers shook his head. 'I would estimate that the nearest land might be several hundred miles to the west. Certainly none anywhere near us, here.'

Derby laughed. 'You ought to be in the Ministry of Information, Withers. You "estimate" it "might" be "several" hundred miles away. Frankly, old man, a mentally retarded Latvian pig-farmer could reckon fairly confidently that the nearest land was between two and three hundred miles west or north-west. Apart from that, I'd say you were dead right.'

'I don't follow you, Derby.'

'Oh. Well, what I mean is this. You said you reckoned we were drifting into the wilderness: into an area which could hardly be described as a Maritime Highway. What I was saying was that on that point we are in complete agreement: we are not heading for any Ocean Cross-roads.'

Withers lowered himself on to the after thwart, and leant forward, resting his head in his hands.

'Flippancy's all very well, Derby, but I think we must face up to the fact that we are in a most serious predicament.'

Derby nudged Mary Lou: his elbow didn't have to travel far.

'Biscuit, please.'

'Coming up!'

101

'Can't I help myself?'

'Not in public.' She handed him one. Withers said stiffly:
'Derby —'

'Oh yes. Sorry. Yes, I agree entirely – a most serious situation, as you say. But for the time being we have food and water, enough for several days, anyway, the boat's more or less dry and there isn't a damn thing we can do about the seriousness of it. Let's go to sleep.'

'One of us should remain awake.' The way he said it, it might have been one of the Ten Commandments.

'What for?'

'In case of emergency. I remained awake, if you remember, last time, and when the storm reached dangerous proportions —'

'I woke up, and found you sitting there, looking at it. Well, stay awake if you want to. I'm going to sleep.'

Mary Lou snuggled up against him.

'Me too.' He told her:

'You feel like a sack of biscuits.'

Derby dreamt that there was to be a party in the depot ship that evening, and he had to have his shower quickly and get dressed, because he was late. It was a most important party for him, because the guest of honour was a famous T.B. specialist who was going to certify that Derby was perfectly fit and could carry on with his duties: Derby was very anxious that this should happen, as it would save him from having to catch the *Gangerolf* which was going to be torpedoed two days out of Subic at considerable inconvenience to her passengers. He stepped under the shower, and found it so pleasant and refreshing that he couldn't force himself to move out again: he stood under it – no damn it, he was lying under it! – and although he desperately wanted to get out and dry himself, his body declined to obey his will. The powerful stream of water seemed to hold him in a sort of spell. Someone was calling: *Come on, Bill!* He thought: That's odd, it's a woman – a woman, in the officers' bathroom! He told her:

102

'Go away! You shouldn't be here – go away!'

'*Bill, wake up!*' He thought: Suppose someone came in here, what'd they think? He shouted over the noise of the shower:

'You'll get into awful trouble!'

'Bill, you're raving. *Do* wake up.'

He woke with Mary Lou shaking his arm and peering at him through the rain. He thought, dully: Oh, it's Mary Lou. Of course, I *did* catch the *Gangerolf*. He realized, too, that he was soaked to the skin: he sat up, stiff as well as wet.

'It's raining.'

She laughed at him. '*Really?* I hadn't noticed. Bill, this isn't rain – it's solid water. I've never seen anything like it . . . I woke you because I thought you ought to start baling again. Oughtn't you?'

'How long's it been doing this?'

'I don't know. I haven't been awake long.'

'Where's Withers?'

She pointed for'ard. 'Over there, somewhere.'

'Have you taken those biscuits out of your shirt?'

'No. Do you think I should?'

'Make an awful soggy mess if you don't. Probably too late now – you'll be encased.' He leant back on his elbows, and yawned. 'It *is* raining hard, isn't it.'

'Don't you think you —'

'I know. Bale . . . I'll go and check up.' He rose wearily and painfully to his feet. Apart from the stiffness of his body, which felt as if it had recently been turned through a mangle, his mouth hurt where the front teeth had gone. He wasn't feeling his best.

Withers was amidships, flat out on his back. Derby leant down and shook him.

'Wake up, Withers.' He sat up immediately. He stared at Derby, then held out his hand, palm up.

'Derby. It's raining.'

'I won't ask you to prove it. But if you'll move, I can get those boards up.'

'What on earth for?'

103

'To check the bilges, old man. See if we need to bale.' He asked, impatiently: 'D'you mind moving?'

Withers shambled aft. Derby knelt down, and prised up the central section of boards. He was relieved to find only a couple of inches of water under them – perhaps three – anyway, nothing to worry about. Presumably it hadn't been raining long before Mary Lou woke up. He went back aft, and told them:

'Dry as a bone.' He had to shout to make himself heard over the drumming noise that the rain made in the boat. Outside, on the sea, it hummed.

Withers pointed easy.

'Dawn. Be light, soon.' There was a greyish streak in the black, and a shine was growing on the surface of the sea. Quite suddenly, as if someone had turned off a tap, the rain had stopped. But the noise of it faded only slowly, and Derby thought: I know how it'll look, when the light comes. He'd seen it before, belts and patches of rain moving over the sea, and if you weren't tied to a straight course you could steer in and out and round them and keep dry. In a drifting lifeboat, you'd have to take it as it came.

The light grew fast out of the sea to the east. It pushed up out of the sea and coloured the sky silver and pink and angry red, and the black sea turned silver grey and shone in streaks that broadened and spread until all the sea was grey. The sky's light spread around the horizon and rose from there to besiege the drifting mass of clouds. Not twenty minutes from that first streak's appearance in the east, you could call it day. The last tinge of colour had gone, it was simply a new day: and at that moment, Withers, who'd been facing west, sprang to his feet.

'Land! Derby, *land*! Two islands, Derby!' Derby studied the banked cloud, the drifting rain patches: between them the air shimmered in wet heat, distorting the line of the horizon. Some of those rain clouds, close to the horizon and seen through the damp haze, could be mistaken easily enough for land. But not, he thought, by any kind of seaman.

'Where old man?'

Withers had lost none of his excitement. Nor had he lowered the pointing hand and arm.

'*There!*' He added: 'You can't see it now.'

'No,' agreed Derby. 'I can't. But that sort of cloud looks very much like land, old man, when it's low on the horizon.'

Withers looked huffed. He stared at Derby, angrily, and waved his hand towards the west.

'In the direction of our drift, Derby, are two small islands. I saw them, a minute ago, quite distinctly. When this rain-storm goes, we'll see them again.'

'I'm sure we will, old man. Mary Lou, how's the biscuit situation?'

She patted herself. 'Confused, I'd say. Want some?'

'Yes. This salt air – makes for appetite.'

Withers stirred himself, and suggested:

'I might try to catch a few fish.'

'How?' Derby asked, frowning. 'What with?' Mary Lou passed him a handful of biscuit: it might have been two, or even three, fused into one soggy lump. He took it from her and examined it without much enthusiasm. She shrugged.

'You don't have to eat it if you don't want to. I won't be hurt.'

'If we could dry it out, it would be rather more attractive. When the sun's up a bit, we could spread it out on the thwarts.' He put it down beside him, and prodded it cautiously with one finger. 'Don't you think so?'

Withers jerked his head towards the bow, and told them, casually: 'Up there, by the anchor cable, there's a boat's bag. A lot of twine and spun-yarn, and some fairly large fish-hooks. There's a palm and needle, too.'

'But that's *marvellous*!' Mary Lou sprang to her feet. 'We can have fish for breakfast! Oh, Withers, you *are* clever!'

Withers smirked. He told her:

'Of course, we can't cook them. But I've been thinking about it, and if we fillet them and lie the fillets out in the sun for a few hours, they'd dry, wouldn't they? Then we could have it with biscuit and it might not be too bad. What do you think?'

'I think you're a genius! Let's start!' They both looked at Derby. He shook his head.

'We haven't any bait.'

'Oh.' Withers stared at him in dismay. 'Of course. I hadn't thought of that.' Mary Lou looked glum, too. Then she brightened up.

'Biscuit! Surely the fish'd go for that?'

'It wouldn't stay on the hook.' Withers pointed at the specimen beside Derby. 'You can see how sloppy it gets when its wet.... You know, Derby, disappointing as this is, it does teach us something.'

'Oh?'

'Certainly. Every boat should have a tin of some sort of fish bait in its equipment. Frankly, I'm surprised it hasn't been thought of before.'

'There, old man, is your entry to the Manual of Seamanship! Jot it down, addressed to Their Lordships, and shove it in a bottle. One day it'll get washed up on some friendly beach and overnight you'll be a posthumous success.'

Withers looked irritated.

'Your flippancy, Derby, contains an element of defeatism.'

Derby laughed. 'Sorry, old man. But I can tell you how to catch fish, now. Just struck me.'

'How?'

'Spinner. We'll cut a strip off the biscuit tin and twist it. Should work a treat.'

'Well, I'm dashed! Derby, you're absolutely right!' He stood up, beaming. 'Let's start, shall we? I'll get the bag.' He hurried forward, almost hurdling the thwarts, and came back with the canvas sack. 'Would you like to make the spinner, Derby?'

'All right.' Derby produced the knife, encrusted with biscuit paste, and began to clean it off. 'Not that I'm much looking forward to raw fish.' Mary Lou reached out, and handed him one of the balers.

'It won't be so bad, Bill, not with biscuit. We could damp the biscuit with water, if it's dry by then, and sort of mix it up with the fish in the middle. It might be absolutely delicious.'

Derby looked at her, and smiled. 'I suppose it might.' He went on looking at her when Withers said:

'Derby.'

'I'm listening, old man.'

'Derby. Would you oblige me by confirming an earlier impression of mine. One which you chose to dismiss summarily, curtly – even rudely? Would you mind looking over there, Derby, at the horizon?'

Derby took his eyes off Mary Lou and stared suspiciously at Withers. The little man had his eyes fixed on the horizon to the west, and that earlier suggestion of a smirk had come to roost on the lower part of his face. Derby rose slowly, and faced west. Withers asked, in a voice that wasn't far from a crow:

'Well, Derby: are those clouds?'

Derby shut his eyes, and opened them again. What they'd seen was still there.

'No. Not clouds ... Not ... Withers, I apologize. But, damn it, it's impossible! It's —'

'It's land, Derby. That's what it is. Two islands!'

'I don't think you're right there, old man. I think it's two mountains or anyway bits of high ground, on one mainland. Isn't there a lower bit connecting them?'

Mary Lou stared at the landfall, too. She asked Derby:

'Is that the way we're drifting?' Derby nodded.

'At the moment, yes. The wind could change, of course, but it's not likely.' Withers shouted, excitedly:

'I think it *is* one bit of land!' He whirled round, delight all over his face. Derby had never seen so much expression on it.

'It seems impossible, Withers. Could be uncharted, I dare say, but surely —'

'Mightn't it be a mirage?' Mary Lou asked. 'One of those things that aren't really there, like oases in the desert?'

'No, honey.' Derby put his arm round her shoulders. 'It's land, all right.' He turned to Withers. 'But even if this wind holds, and the current, it'll be a long time before we get that far. Might as well begin persecuting those fish.'

The island loomed larger as the day wore on. The sun climbed and threw down its heat and dried the biscuit and made the raw fillets of fish warm, and the warmth increased and propagated their natural smell. There were many kinds of fish, all small and none of them recognizable. Long after they had enough in the boat for at least three days' food, Withers continued hauling in new ones: he insisted that, later on, they'd be glad of them.

Mary Lou split the fish open, removed those parts which looked as though they might be edible, in time, and dropped the remnants over the side. Quite frequently she washed her hands in the sea.

Soon, all the thwarts were covered with strips of drying fish. Astern, in the boat's wake, gulls of many shapes and sizes squawked and shrieked while they gorged themselves, and then lay, silent, swollen and supine in the placid, littered wake.

Derby, who'd been asleep, woke and screwed his face into an expression of disgust.

'The stench of that offal, old man, is utterly repulsive. Don't you think you have enough?'

Withers didn't even turn his head. He'd had a bite and he was dragging the line in, hand over hand.

'*Can't* have enough, Derby. Suppose the fish stop biting? They might you know.'

Derby nodded. He closed his eyes and murmured:

'I wish to God they would.'

By afternoon they could hear the thunder of the surf, and make out some of the details of the island. Wind and tide were moving them fast towards it, and the three of them sat in silence as they watched what they imagined would be their future home growing closer and higher. Certainly it looked as though they'd end up on its shore.

'You were absolutely right, Derby.'

'Was I?'

'About it being one island. I must say, I thought you were mistaken. I'd have sworn it was two.'

Approaching as they were from the east, or slightly north of east, the island's silhouette was that of two steep hills joined at their bases by a narrow strip of land not far above sea level. The steeper hill was the right-hand one, and from this distance it seemed to be densely wooded, while the southern heights had more gentle slopes and fewer trees. At sea level, the whole length of the island was white with surf.

Withers turned to Derby, and told him happily: 'There doesn't seem to be any reef. Beach all along. We're in luck.'

'Goody!' Mary Lou asked: 'That'll be easier, won't it?'

Derby shook his head, and pointed.

'Look there, under the peak of that northern hill, just about in line with that. Looks like a string of rocks. See?'

'Can't say I do, Derby.' Withers was shielding his eyes against the sun. 'Where?'

'I may be wrong. But if you take a line down vertically from that hill-top, where it'd hit the coastline looks like a rock headland. Get it?'

After a minute Withers muttered: 'It could be, Derby. I dare say it could be.'

'Then train left along the surf line. Just in line with the valley, I think the rocks end. I'd say there was a promontory of rock curving out horn-shaped and ending or submerging there.'

'I can't see it, Derby. You may be right, but —'

'Where I said, where the rocks seem to be, the surf's higher, breaking over them. See that bit of rainbow? That's spray. And from the low bit, almost right to the left edge of the island, I reckon I can see beach above the surf.' He had to look away, and blink the water out of his eyes. The sun was just about over the north edge of the island, lowering into the west, and it took a lot of looking into. But he was quite sure that he was right. Withers couldn't see it, but then Withers was a General Service man, and surface sailors never learnt to use their eyes as submariners did. Submariners so often had their lives depending on their eyesight that they acquired the habit of getting the most out of them. It was seeing the enemy or a sign of the enemy before he saw you that made the killings and

109

kept you alive to do it again. He told Withers:

'It isn't so good.'

'What d'you mean, Derby?'

'The line of our drift is at those rocks. Look, old man, it's quite clear now. *Look*.'

Withers peered at the island with his eyes screwed up and his mouth slightly open. He nodded.

'I dare say you're right, Derby.' Mary Lou asked:

'What happens if we do drift on to those rocks, Bill?' He looked at her. She wasn't at all frightened, not that he could see. She was just interested, wanting information. He decided not to tell her anything of the power of sea breaking on a reef.

'Depends how we hit. Generally speaking, this hooker'll stick there and get beaten into splinters fairly rapidly. We'll nip out and swim to the beach. But you see, when we get close in and meet the backwashes and suchlike that you get from rocks and beaches, the drift of the current may change entirely and take us past them. Could take us right clear of the island.'

'Oh, I do hope it won't!'

He laughed. 'Like the look of the place? You want to live there?' She nodded, eagerly.

'I think it'd be *fun*!'

He could see that she really did think so. She had some of a child's mentality inside the body of an exceptionally attractive woman. Not for the first time, he felt her warmth meeting his own psychological and sexual antennae. He told himself, sternly: Derby, old man, keep your mind on the job or it'll end up on the rocks.

Suddenly she leapt to her feet, pointing.

'Bill! *Bill!*' It was almost a shriek. 'Bill, look!' He looked in the direction of her pointing finger and gasped.

'Well, I'm damned!'

Withers blinked at them both, glanced quickly at the island and looked back at Derby.

'What – what are you —'

'Just look, old man. From the right peak, two fingers left. See that smoke?'

Withers turned back to the island, shielding his eyes with both hands. Derby put out his left hand, and took Mary Lou's: they sat close together, staring at the thin column of blue smoke that was rising from the far side of the hill's left flank.

VIII

The roar of the surf was deafening, terrifying. The boat floated only about twenty yards short of the long jagged spur of rock, and the rollers (rising higher and stronger at every moment as they neared the point) lifted her and drove her forward at the waiting menace. From this closeness the rocks towered high above them and the sea hurling itself thundering against the barrier flung up a curtain of spray which hung there all the time with the rainbow slanting across it's top. Behind that loomed the bulk of the island, tall and deep green but turning darker, almost black, at the edges, with the sun dipping down behind.

For the moment, the island was of secondary interest: the rocks held all their attention. Withers stared at them in helpless fear, as though he'd given up any idea of helping himself and now it was all in the rocks' hands: all he could do was crouch there in the boat and watch them coming and wonder if they'd let him live. In the stern, Derby fought with the rudder: there was no tiller to work it with, and he hung over the stern using every ounce of his strength to control it with his hands grasping the top of the rudder itself. It wasn't easy, he could hardly get any purchase on it at all, and his efforts were of little value anyway because in the swirl and rush and drag of surface water even a properly manageable rudder would have been almost useless. But it was better than doing nothing.

Mary Lou sat wide-eyed in excitement: she kept looking at Derby and back again at the rocks as if she was wondering why he didn't simply swing the thing over and steer the boat clear. They were close now and the spray was soaking, thick and continuous. Derby shouted:

'Come aft! Both of you!' Mary Lou came back immediately and sat herself on the stern thwart. But Withers didn't move.

'Withers!' He was shouting in competition with the sea. Withers glanced round over his shoulder, and immediately looked away again.

'Come aft, blast you!'

'Why?' His shout was a high yelp of fear, and his face was as white as the deep salt froth on the water. 'Better here, Derby, to jump out when we hit the rocks!'

Derby used a word he usually avoided: he spat it at the spray as if he'd been wanting to get rid of it for some time. He let go of the rudder, flung himself for'ard, grabbed Withers round the waist and dragged him aft like a sack of potatoes. He deposited him, screaming with fear and with anger, on the thwart beside Mary Lou.

'You're mad, Derby! You wait, I'll have you —'

'Shut up!' Derby grabbed the rudder head, and forced it over. The rocks weren't ten yards ahead, the very point of that vicious curve was waiting for them, sharp as a dog's tooth and as white, and in the violence of the broken surging sea it was all he could do to move the rudder an inch. But he got it over. He called: 'Mary Lou?' He had his eyes on the point of rock and all his weight on the rudder.

'Yes, Bill?' For a moment he couldn't talk to her. Then he shouted:

'You too, Withers. . . . We'll stay right aft here until the last moment, so the bow'll be high when she strikes. Then when I tell you and not before, run like hell straight up the boat and on to the rock as high as you can get. All right?'

'All right, Bill.'

'She may swing round and hit beam on. In that case we'll get thrown out. Just get up on the rocks as best you can.'

'I'll be all right.'

He thought: She doesn't realize that the barnacles on those rocks are perfectly capable of removing the side of her face, if she gets washed against them once. She's a delightfully un-imaginative lass. He told Withers, shouting over the roar of the sea:

'If you try to get out before I tell you, I'll wring your bloody neck!' Withers shot him a terrified and at the same time malevolent glance: Derby thought: I'll hear about this, on the beach. He shouted: 'Hold tight!'

The sea took the boat like a matchstick and flung it at the end of the rocks. The crash that had to come was a yard – three seconds – ahead of her raised and rushing bow when the wave's backwash swept down and stopped her dead, throwing the bow off to port and away from the rocks' point: a second later another wave rolled up under her stern and while Derby fought the rudder with his hands burning and the sweat pouring down his face the new force swept the boat past the rocks. He thought dazedly: 'We're clear – it's a ruddy miracle! Mary Lou screamed:

'Bill, you're *wonderful*!' He glanced at her, saw her face all shiny wet with salt spray and her eyes alight with excitement: she threw herself at him, and kissed him on the mouth. The wave rushed on from under them and the boat crashed down on solid rock.

It was the falling, submerged end of the point. Withers shot for'ard and threw himself over the bow into the smoothly rolling water ahead of them.

Derby looked down, and found Mary Lou lying in the stern-sheets looking up at him. She looked surprised. He'd been pushing her gently off his lap when the boat had struck, and that further impetus had sent her flying. He looked beyond her, to where he expected to see rock and salt water forcing up through the bottom boards: but the boat seemed dry and intact. For a moment she was almost balanced on the sloping spine of the rock, then as the wave drained off she slumped to port until it seemed she'd roll all the way over: but just as the list reached danger point and he was thinking of telling Mary Lou to swim for it, the boat's keel began to slide down over that invisible rock slope.

Only seconds later the boat was floating evenly with the swell driving her gently towards the beach. The pound of the surf on the rocks was background music, now, instead of present danger: the water in here was smooth and placid. Just ahead of the boat, Withers was swimming for his life.

Mary Lou pointed at him, and pealed with laughter. Derby

looked, and chuckled too. Withers was only a few feet from the bow, splashing and gasping: now he turned his distorted face, and saw them. At once he reversed his floundering course, and struggled spluttering to the boat's side, where he grabbed hold of the gun'l and began trying to pull himself aboard. But the gun'l was too high, and he hadn't the strength. All he could do was jerk about in the water, rocking the boat and groaning as if he was in some sort of pain.

Mary Lou, still laughing, moved forward, intending to help him aboard. Derby stopped her.

'Mary Lou.'

She turned and looked at him questioningly, and he shook his head and patted the thwart where she'd been sitting. She sat down.

Withers interrupted his groans long enough to call:

'Derby, give me a hand up!' Derby rose slowly, crossed over and looked down at Withers. He looked like a white rat, half-drowned.

'No, Withers, I won't. You chose to swim, and you can bloody well swim.'

Withers called, frantically: 'Mary Lou! *Please* come and help me! I can't hold on much longer! I'll drown!'

She glanced uncertainly at Derby, then stood up and came towards them. Derby snapped:

'Mary Lou. Go back there and sit down, unless you want me to put you over the side with him.' She shrugged, and went back. Derby spluttered on a high note:

'Derby! You're countermanding my orders! I'm the senior officer, I'll —'

'You're mistaken, Withers. *I* am in charge of this boat. The previous senior officer abandoned his command in a manner which I would prefer not to discuss' – he pointed at Mary Lou – 'in the presence of a rating. . . . He decided to swim, and as far as I'm concerned that's what he's doing.'

'You'll regret this, Derby!'

'I doubt it, old man.' He went back aft, and sat down at Mary Lou's side. Shielding his eyes, he took stock of the beach ahead of them.

They were still forty, perhaps fifty yards from the water's edge, but the boat was moving fast now and they'd soon be in the surf. There was a lot of it, piling up and breaking hard and deep across the shallows. It'd be a tricky landing. Derby pointed at the surf, and told Mary Lou:

'If we aren't pretty careful, this craft'll swing into that lot beam-on and capsize.'

'Does it matter? I mean, we'll be there, won't we? I don't mind getting wet, if that's what you're thinking of.'

'Nothing so gallant, honey. But we may need this boat, and what's more I don't want to lose our water barrels ... I wonder how long that anchor cable is?'

He clambered for'ard, and began to sort it out of the heap around the anchor. Withers stared at him imploringly.

'Derby, a joke's a joke, but dash it —'

'I'm not joking, old man.'

He flaked the cable out, up and down the length of the boat, over the top of the thwarts. Then he lifted the anchor and put it ready on the bow thwart. He checked that the other end of the cable was well secured to the shackle in the bows, then he came back aft and sat down.

'We'll let her drift quite a bit closer. Don't want to run out of rope, close to the beach.'

Mary Lou asked him quietly:

'Don't you think you ought to let him in?'

'Why? The little brute left us in the lurch, didn't he? Teach him to save his blasted skin, this will.'

'Bill, we've got to live together on this island. It'll be easy enough to get on each others' nerves later on. I think we ought to start off on the right foot, not squabbling.'

He looked away from her, at the beach and up to the start of the trees, palms at first dotted here and there, thickening inland and changing to other, denser timber on the higher slopes. And just as he looked there, he caught a glimpse of the figure of a man disappearing at a run into the trees. It was so quick that a second later he wasn't even sure that he'd seen it: certainly no details of the creature's appearance had registered in his mind. He went on staring at the trees where the man had vanished, thinking: It was a man, all right, I'm sure it was a man. What colour it was, or whether it had worn clothes, he had no idea.

Mary Lou broke into his bewilderment.

'Have you seen a ghost, or something?'

'Eh? Oh, sorry. I was just – looking.'

'Gaping, you mean. Bill, *do* help that little wretch out of the water.' He nodded, and stood up. He thought: She's right, we'd better stick together. From somewhere at the back of his mind a premonition told him that their life on this island was going to have its complications without any of their own making. He went for'ard. Withers groaned:

'Derby —'

'All right, old man. Hand.' He took the claw that rose and dragged its owner into the boat.

'Thank you, Derby. Thank you.' Limp and panting like an old dog on a hot day, Withers told him: 'I don't blame you, Derby, I'm sorry I left you like that. But you see, it seemed to me that to lighten the boat quickly would —'

'You were probably right, old man. . . . Look, I'm going to drop the hook and kedge her in stern first. We don't want to capsize.'

'No. Of course not. A jolly good idea, Derby.' He pointed at the flaked cable. 'I see you've got it all ready.'

' 'm. Look, I'd like to show you.' He led Withers up to the bow, where he could talk without Mary Lou hearing. He didn't want to worry the girl unnecessarily. 'Withers. You remember that smoke we saw?'

'Yes. Yes, Derby?'

'A moment ago I saw a man in those trees up there. Now, look. It could be some unfriendly lot of wogs. Even Japs. In any case, I'd like to get a look at them rather than we sit around and let them check up on *us*.'

'I agree with you entirely, Derby. I have always maintained that attack is the best defence.'

'You have, have you?' Derby couldn't help smiling. 'Well, listen. When we've beached the boat, we'll take the barricoes, and your fish too, I suppose, and find some sheltered spot

117

where we can settle down for the night. It'll be dark, soon. Then I'd be grateful if you'd stay and look after Mary Lou while I perform a swift recce. I may be able to pick up that fellow's tracks.'

'Certainly, Derby! An excellent plan. You can rely on me entirely.'

'I'm glad to hear that. Well —' He shot a glance at the surf line: another forty feet, and they'd be in it. 'Would you nip aft, and unship the rudder, old man?'

Withers went aft without another word. Derby lifted the anchor, and dropped it over the bow. The rope ran out fast and when it stopped he paid out another couple of fathoms and took a turn around the for'ard thwart. The strain came on the rope and he backed the turn up with his weight while the anchor held the bow and the boat began to swing until her stern pointed at the beach. He called to the others to join him in the bow, and began to let the cable out foot by foot, keeping the strain on all the time while the boat edged stern first into the surf. She pitched a bit and rolled, but she couldn't broach-to with the kedge holding her bow, and presently, without any trouble except some skin off Derby's hands, her stern grated on the sand. Derby told them, pointing:

'Over the stern, please.'

They scrambled down the boat and with their weight in the stern the boat grounded hard, but they jumped over into the surf and she was light again at once and drove on higher. Derby walked aft, holding the rope tight in his hands as he went; then he dropped it, and joined them in the swirling water. It was only knee deep. As soon as his weight left the boat's stern, her bow began to swing around, but he and Withers lifted the stern and dragged her up as far as they could. Mary Lou stood on the beach wriggling her toes in the sand and watching with a smile on her face as Derby climbed back into the boat and brought the barricoes out. He handed them down to Withers, one by one, and Withers caried them up the beach and set them down out of the sea's reach. After he'd taken them both up, he came back again, and Derby said:

118

'I suppose you've come for that stinking heap of fish?'

Withers nodded. 'I know it smells, Derby. But it may be our only food, we don't know that there's anything edible here. I think we should keep it, just in case.'

Derby handed him the boat's bag.

'We can catch more fish, old man. I'm afraid I dropped yours, over the side. I slipped. Terribly sorry.'

It was over the shoulder of the northern hill that the smoke column had appeared, and it was on the lower slopes of that hill that Derby had seen the man running. So he led his party to the left, up the other slope from the beach into the palms and left around the lower contours of the hill. He walked ahead, carrying the untapped barrico: behind him Withers lurched and staggered under the weight of the other one, and Mary Lou had the boat's bag. As he walked, Derby looked to right and left for signs of life, human or animal. But there were none: only an occasional seagull drifted down over the tree-tops, squawking as it passed. The three of them shuffled along in single file, looking around them with mixed interest and anxiety as the light faded and shadows deepened under the trees. Mary Lou called softly:

'Where're we going, Bill? Trip round the isalnd?'

'Just up here a bit. Somewhere we can shelter for the night. Tired?'

'I'm all right.' She stopped, and called excitedly: 'Bill! what about *there*?' He turned, and followed her pointing arm with his eyes. She was pointing uphill, through the palms: there, just below the start of thicker trees and bushes, was a sort of shelf, like a wide, shallow bunker in a golf course. The back wall of it looked vertical, and thick clumps of something like casuarina, backed by palms, overhung the miniature cliff.

'Let's have a look.' He swung right, up through the palms; the others headed uphill, too, and they converged on the sheltered bunker. Derby nodded, and set his barrico down on the sand. 'All right, Withers?'

Withers panted: 'Excellent, I should say. I dare say we

shall find some much more satisfactory spot tomorrow, of course. Eh, Derby?'

'Indubitably, old man.'

Mary Lou lay down on her back and pulled the boat's bag under her head as a pillow: but she sat up again, quickly, and pushed it away.

'What on earth's in that thing?' Derby told her:

'The lines and stuff, and my knife, and the rest of the biscuits and the two halves of the tin. They'll come in handy for cooking and collecting water, later on.'

She lay flat out on the sand and closed her eyes. She told him, lazily:

'This sand's lovely and soft. Like a great big feather bed. Come and try it.' She smiled up at him. Withers coughed.

'Derby. Shall we have a drink of water and a biscuit all round, now, or would you rather wait until you've —'

'Let's have a snack.' He'd been thinking: By the time I get to those tracks, it'll be pitch dark, and I won't see them. Besides, I haven't a clue about how the land lies and in the dark I'll be at a ridiculous disadvantage. Better sit the night out here, and start exploring at first light. He told Mary Lou:

'I didn't think it'd get dark so quickly ... I'd arranged with Withers that he'd look after you while I tootled off and checked up on that smoke we saw. But I think, Withers, it'd be a bit pointless now.'

'I should think it *would*!' Mary Lou sat up and began brushing the fine sand out of her hair. 'Just you *dare* run off and leave us all alone! Come on, let's eat.' She opened the bag and put one of the balers on the sand beside her and fished out the biscuits one by one and put them in the tin. She said: 'They look absolutely scrumptious!' Derby sat down beside her.

'I've known better.' She glanced at him, then giggled and peered down the front of her shirt, holding it out at the neck. She shook her head.

'Sorry. None of that kind left. You gourmet, you.'

Withers used his cough again. Derby thought: I can summon that dry hawk at will. Withers did it again and suggested:

'Shall we have a ration of water all round, before we start eating? Or would you prefer to wait and have it later?'

Mary Lou made a snorting sound, and stared rudely at him.

'Ration? What *do* you mean? We're on land, now – let's swallow the lot.' Withers frowned. He told her:

'We have not as yet discovered any supply of water on this island. For all we know, there may be none at all. Please understand me, the last thing I wish to do is to alarm you: all I say is that until we are sure of our future supplies we should – er – go easy.' He glanced at Derby for confirmation.

'He's right, Mary Lou. We'd better stick to the single swig system.'

She shrugged her shoulders. 'All right. But I think it's silly. How do all these trees live if there isn't any water?'

'Water underground, honey, and rain. But we're neither moles nor locusts.' She looked annoyed.

'Are you sure you aren't? I'm beginning to wonder.'

Withers took the other baler out of the bag, and poured water into it out of the barrico they'd been using before.

'You first.' He handed the tin to Mary Lou. She poured the water into her mouth out of one corner of the tin.

'It tastes salty. You should have washed it out.' Withers poured again, this time for Derby.

'Yours, Derby.' He handed it over and Derby drank quickly and handed the tin back. Withers poured his own. Mary Lou pointed at him, and announced, sternly:

'You're cheating.'

'I – I beg your pardon?'

'You gave yourself four glugs, and we only got three!'

'*Glugs?*'

'Yes, glugs! Each time water comes out of the hole it glugs. I've counted them: we've had three each and you've taken four.'

'I'm sure you're mistaken, young woman. I am going by the depth of water on the tin, not glugs. You're making a most grave accusation, a most serious —'

'*Sh!*' Derby hissed at them for silence: he was on his knees, listening. He put one finger to his lips, then whispered, very quietly: 'Something moving in the bushes. He pointed at the trees to their left, the falling ground. He whispered to them: 'Get back in the shadow.'

Mary Lou slithered back against the sand and gravel wall, and Withers crawled there on his hands and knees.

'What – what d'you rhink it is, Derby?'

Derby didn't answer. He crept to the left edge of the embankment: he kept close to the ground, and well inside the shadow of the overhang, and he peered over the edge, straining his eyes downhill into the less than half light.

A bush moved, and Derby stiffened. He thought: Did I imagine that? From long hours on a submarine's bridge in enemy waters at night, he knew how easy it is to see what you're looking for when it isn't there. No, he thought, I'm sure it moved: but this is all very well, there could be a dozen more of them, whoever they are, on the other side, or above us, Nothing in front, anyway, the sand gleamed white and empty between the trunks of the palms. Down there, in front, there'd hardly be cover for a snake.

The only sound was the constant hum of the surf and a more distant booming from the reef. It was so quiet, here among the trees, that he felt his own breathing was interfering with his hearing, so he rested his chin on his hands on the edge of the embankment and held his breath.

He heard the bush rustle. There wasn't any wind to move it. He stared intently through the growing dark, and saw a part of the bush's vague mass detaching itself towards the left. He forced all his concentration into his eyes, watching that slow and shadowy movement, and, quite suddenly, he saw without any doubt at all that it was a man creeping slowly uphill from right to left. Derby thought: Once he gets round on our flank and above us, we can't do a damn thing. There's only one thing to do and the only time I can do it is *now*.

He flung himself forward, across the slope, stooping and running as hard as he could go, and dived headlong at the intruder. He, taken by surprise and off-balance, had half-risen from his knees: Derby crashed into him, grabbing him round the neck, and they hit the ground with a crash which brought shrieks of alarm from some night-fowl overhead which had hitherto kept silent. The man struggled frantically and tore at Derby's face with hands like claws. He got his thumbs into Derby's eyes and dug hard and it hurt, but Derby cracked his forehead down like a hammer into the man's face and the grip relaxed. Derby leant sideways, screwing his elbow viciously into the strange neck, and after a moment the body under him went limp. Quickly Derby shifted his hold: he put his left hand firmly round the throat and his right on the man's left wrist, twisting the arm back into a position which he knew, only too well from his boyhood at Dartmouth, to be extremely painful. The body quivered, and groaned in pain. Then it spoke.

'Okay, okay. Guess I'm all in.'

Derby couldn't believe his ears. He knew that voice well! He leant down, and peered through the dark, and while the face he saw was thinner and had a couple of days' beard on it, there wasn't any doubt who it belonged to. Derby let go, and sat back. A pressure rose inside him, he couldn't hold it in. He threw his head back and roared with laughter. Once he'd let it start, it was difficult to stop.

Withers called, nervously:

'Derby? Are you all right?' Mary Lou echoed:

'Bill, darling, are you all right?' He stifled his laughter, and rose shakily to his feet. He called:

'Withers – Mary Lou – come down here. It's *Spatter*!'

IX

'Say, Commander, might I have just one more sip out the barrel?' Withers looked at Derby, and Spatter added: 'Fact is, that was the first drink o' clean water I had me in two days.'

Withers passed him the barrico. 'A small one, mind. We don't yet know what water there is here on the island. Have you seen any, Spatter?'

'Sure, I have. Tastes kinda salty, but it's okay, I guess.' He pointed south. 'Li'l stream running down thataway. Fact is, th' Krauts're camped right on it, low down where I was tellin' ya.' He drank deeply, and passed the barrel back. 'Thanks, Commander. Sure is fine, pure water.' He lay back on the sand, wincing at the pain in his ricked neck. His nose wasn't bleeding now: at one time they'd thought it would never stop.

'Well, now. As I was sayin', the Nips reckon they can't accommodate all the Krauts, so one officer 'n' nine men gets back in them floats, an' soon as the sub dives I climb in, too. Funny, none of 'em seems to mind me being along, then, and Leutnant Kreisch, that's the officer, he talks English pretty good too, why, he's darned amiable. Sure is kinda different now! Way I see it, them Krauts is just as goddamn happy as I am that they ain't been shot up, like it seemed they was going to be, an' in consequence I'm right with them sorta, one o' the boys. Tell y'another thing: I reckon that shootin' kinda shook 'em, they reckon we're just so many white men that th' monkeys ain't shot.

'Well. Them li'l rafts is uncomfortable as all hell, but they drift faster'n you'd credit. An' as soon as we get on dry land, the Krauts turn nasty. On the beach, Kreisch makes a speech, kinda, in German, and shouts "Heil Hitler" and all that stuff, then he tells me in English this is German territory an' I'm their prisoner. Well, I say to him, Lootenant, I say, you're talking outa turn, boy. You guys is my prisoners, ever since you got yourselves fixed up by th' U.S. Navy. Know what he did?'

'What did he do, Spatter, old man?' Derby was lying on his belly with his chin propped on his fists and his eyes on the dark shape of Spatter. 'What did he do?'

'Knocked me down, that's what. Tell ya. I taken a hell of a beating, f' one day.' Spatter rubbed his neck, gingerly. 'I sure have. So he knocks me down an' a coupla his fellers start jumpin' up an' down on me. Kreisch tells 'em: Lay off the guy, will ya? He asks me: Are we your prisoners, Herr Captain? Well, not wantin' no more third degree, I tell him, Lootenant, I guess you ain't. Then a bunch of th' other Krauts start talking an' jeerin', lookin' at me, an' Kreisch asks me do I know what them guys is sayin'? No, I tell him, I don't understand no goddam languages 'cept Uncle Sam's. Kreisch tells me: They're saying if you make any goddam trouble maybe I'll let 'em cook you f'a week's fresh meat.'

Withers told him, with an air of authority: 'That would be contrary to the Hague Convention.'

'I guess you're right, Commander. But this feller Kreisch ain't the conventional type. No, sir. . . . Well, I helps 'em tote all the rafts up into the hillside, under the trees, and —'

'Why'd they want to do that?' Derby's voice came sharply out of the dark.

'Seems the Krauts that got took into the sub promised they'd call up another one to search this whole goddam area. Kreisch reckons on gettin' picked up inside a week, an' he aims t' use them rafts for when the sub comes.'

Mary Lou spoke for the first time in an hour.

'But that's awful!'

Derby told her: 'I don't think so. Christiansen would've got an SOS and an enemy report out before he abandoned ship. There'll be a search from our side, too.'

Spatter didn't sound so cheerful about it.

'Maybe, Commander. But Kreisch reckons to get picked up most any time now. He ain't reckonin' on any long stay here. An' see, if the sub that comes is a Nip, an' I wouldn't know what else it'd be, well, we seen Nips, huh, th' way they act with prisoners? That's why I beat it, soon's I got a chance when the Krauts got settled down makin' a fire an' cuttin' wood and this 'n' that. I lit out, but fast. An' I been dodgin' the basstuds all day. I ain't anxious to be around when the Nips is. No sir, I ain't.... Look, Commander, lemme show y' a thing.'

He dragged a Mauser pistol out of the pocket of his tattered trousers, and held it up close in front of Derby's face. The others leaned close to see what it was. Derby whistled.

'I'm glad you didn't use that on me, Spatter.'

'Yeah. One bullet, that's all I have, just one. I took this off one o' my enlisted men, in the water, after he'd been shot. I've been reckonin' on keepin' this bullet for me, see, if the Nips get too goddam close.'

Withers held out his hand. He said:

'Spatter. I am the senior allied officer on this island. Give me that weapon.'

'Now see here, Commander —'

'Captain Spatter, that is an order. Give me your pistol.'

'Hell, Commander —'

'Spatter! — Your pistol! ... Thank you.' Withers slipped it into his own pocket. 'You say it contains only one bullet?'

'That's right. But goddam it, Commander, I'd —'

'No doubt you are wondering why I insist on taking charge of this firearm ... Very well, I shall explain. Mary Lou, ever since this officer informed us of the presence of a superior enemy force on the island, I have been thinking of your safety. From Captain Spatter's description of their behaviour, it is evident to me that they are disorderly, undisciplined and – er – hostile. *You*, Wren Smith, are a woman.'

Mary Lou giggled and Derby had to laugh, too. She asked Withers:

'You guessed that, so soon, Commander Witheringham?'

Spatter said: 'I guess he found some goddam textbook.'

'Please.' Withers wasn't amused. 'This is no laughing matter, gentlemen. Wren Smith, as a woman, is in considerable danger.'

'You mean, my – my honour?'

'Precisely. As the senior officer of this party, I shall take it upon myself, with the help of this pistol and its one bullet, to ensure your safety.'

Mary Lou gasped. 'Commander Witheringham! If you have some old-world idea in your head that I would prefer death to – to anything else – I'd better tell you here and now to forget it!'

Derby began to laugh again. He patted Mary Lou on her shoulder.

'*That's* my girl!'

Withers snapped: 'Derby!'

'Sorry, old man.'

'My intention is as follows. Tomorrow morning, under a flag of truce, I shall approach the enemy camp and interview their officer. I shall then take steps to negotiate a permanent truce, and I shall warn him that I will personally shoot any man who – approaches – that is, who —'

'Tries to rape me?'

Withers coughed. He said: 'I shall endeavour to make my meaning clear without being unnecessarily offensive or – er – vulgar.'

It must have been at about two or three in the morning that Derby woke. At first he thought somebody was shining a torch in his face, and he rolled over on to his side, blinking, to save his eyes from that direct and savage light. There was a hand on his arm, light but firm, its fingers pressing evenly into his biceps.

'Bill!'

It was Mary Lou. She was close beside him, whispering into his ear: that light came from the moon, not from any torch. It was a brilliant silver, and against it the palms over their heads were jet black and strikingly beautiful. Suddenly, he was wide awake. He turned his head to face her, wondering why she'd woken him, and she leant closer and kissed him. At first he started to pull back, but she slid her hands round behind his head with their fingers interlocked and after the first backward start he didn't try to take his mouth off hers. Quite suddenly this had nothing to do with their ordinary living or the world of daylight, with their names or initials or the fact that he was married, and in love with his wife: that was some separate existence and it had no connection with this. All that well-used scenery had been whipped up out of sight and caring and they were alone on a deep empty stage against a wide cyclorama composed of sand and moons and palms: the orchestra was the surf along the beach.

She leant back with her face an inch from his and whispered quietly so the others wouldn't hear and wake:

'I'd like to go for a walk, Bill. Coming?'

He told himself: Bill Derby, you're sticking your head in a noose. You'll regret this, old man. He told her:

'You go first. If they don't wake up, I'll follow.' He watched them while she slid away as quietly as a ghost into the black palm trunks; Withers was snoring on his back, and Spatter lay in a grotesque sprawl on the other side of him. Neither of them stirred. Derby almost hoped they would, but they didn't, and he told himself: You've had it, you're no damn good any more. He rose to his feet, watching carefully to see that he'd throw no shadow over Withers's face. Then he walked slowly downhill to where Mary Lou was waiting for him on the edge of the trees.

Withers woke him at first light.

'Derby! Wake up! It's light!'

'It's been light all night.' He sat up, and glanced at Mary Lou: she was sleeping curled on her side, with her knees up, and there was a faint smile on her face. Derby thought: I'm not only a four-letter man, I'm a bloody fool, and that's infinitely worse. But he looked down through the trees at the beach, and he couldn't help smiling, too. Suddenly he saw the tracks they'd made in the sand.

'Withers, old man, I'm going for a swim.' He jumped to his feet and ran down over the line of the footmarks to the beach, swung right, and, in a place where the sand had been disturbed and scattered, flung himself down and removed his shoes. He went into the water wearing his shorts. He splashed about in the shallows and rubbed the water over his body, and he'd turned and was wading back up to the beach when Mary Lou came running down over the same tracks and sat down beside his shoes. She called:

'You *clever* old thing!' He frowned at her and shook his head, advising caution, and she laughed at him. 'I meant, clever to think of a swim before breakfast.' He was up beside her, now, dripping, and she murmured: 'Can I go in bare?'

'No. Withers wouldn't like it.'

'He would really ... Bill, this *is* a good idea: we can always come here, now.'

'No, Mary Lou. We can't.'

'You think it's too close?'

'I'm talking about – the whole thing, not the place.' She looked at him, and laughed.

'You *poor* old thing, you! Not at your best in the morning, are you?'

Still laughing, she walked slowly down to the sea. He pushed his feet into his shoes and shuffled uphill. He thought: I must have been out of my mind! And now she – oh, hell! Somewhere behind his recognition of the situation's hazards and impossibility he had a warmly pleasant idea that she wasn't going to let him get out of this thing he'd started. He fought that, told himself that if he didn't get out of it now he'd never be able to later on.

'Refreshed, Derby? Invigorated? Ready for a biscuit?' Derby sat down, and nodded at Spatter who was sitting up and rubbing sand off his knuckles into his eyes.

'Morning, Spatter.' He told Withers: 'Yes, thank you.' Withers passed him a biscuit.

'I'll catch some fish today, Derby. And I dare say we'll find some palms with coconuts on them. Perhaps we shall come across mangoes, pawpaws, and – er – fruits of that sort. Have you come across any, Spatter?'

'Can't say I have, Commander. But then, I guess I weren't

looking for 'em either. Wouldn't know 'em of I did see 'em, I guess. Gimme one o' them cookies, Commander.'

Mary Lou came back, and Withers rose politely to his feet. She walked past him, and threw herself down beside Derby. He handed her a biscuit, and she took it in her teeth out of his hand. In a muffled voice she said:

'Thanks, lover boy!' He started, and Withers began to clear his throat: it sounded like a short burst from a dentist's drill.

'I trust you slept well – er – Mary Lou?' She told him, smiling: 'I had a disturbed night.' Derby glared at her, and Withers said, cheerily:

'I'm so sorry. Personally, I slept like a top. Well, Derby, are we ready? Eh?'

'Uh? Ready for what, old man?'

'I'd like you to come with me to meet this German chap. I thought I'd remove my shirt, and you could carry it, you see.' Derby stared at him.

'Have you gone mad?'

'Tied to a pole, or something . . . As a flag of truce, Derby.'

'Oh, I see. Yes, all right. Where's the pole?'

'I'll find one. There must be lots of them about.'

Mary Lou said: 'I'd like a drink of water, please.'

'Of course.' Withers wrenched the bung out of the barrel. 'A short drink each, eh?' He passed the barrel over and went pottering off among the trees: presently he came back with the central part of a fallen palm frond. He pulled his shirt off over his head, and secured it by its arms to the green tapering wood.

'Here you are, Derby. Shall we proceed?'

'Haven't had my swig yet, old man.'

'Ah. For that matter, neither have I.' Derby took the barrel from Spatter, and drank, and then passed it on to Withers. When Withers had swallowed his mouthful, he said: 'I should say there was very little water remaining in this.'

Spatter asked: 'We got another there, huh?'

'Certainly, Spatter.' Withers was in a genial mood, this morning. He beamed at everybody before he spoke. 'But I think we should retain that for use in emergency. After I have seen the German – what did you say his name was?'

'Kreisch.'

'Yes. After our talk, we will embark upon a preliminary exploration of the island. Well, Derby – ready?' Derby nodded, and stood up. Spatter said:

'If I'm watching *this* end, Commander, you'd best leave me the Mauser.'

'I can hardly do that, Spatter. I intend to display it, to the Germans. Otherwise, you see, they might suspect that I was simply – er – bluffing. Come, Derby.'

They headed north, parallel to the shore, and soon the ground dipped sharply into the valley which separated the two hills. There were fewer palms here, and the sand was harder: it was really a sand strip linking the two beaches, and it occurred to Derby that in heavy weather it might well be under water.

They slanted left and began to climb the shoulder of the northern rise. Derby stopped.

'Withers, we'd do better to keep to the low ground. Over to the other side, then turn north along the coast. It'll be easier going, and we'll stay in the open instead of suddenly blundering out of the trees at them.'

'Very well, Derby. You had better raise the flag.'

Derby lifted it. The frond bent over under the weight of the shirt, and the shirt hung limply in the still, hot air. It didn't look much like a flag.

They came out on to the southern end of the west beach. It was wider, but not as long as their own, and although today the sea was dead flat there was no reef to break the waves' force. Withers said:

'I think our choice of coast is the better, don't you?' Derby didn't answer: looking up the slopes in a north-easterly direction he could see a circle of sprawled figures and a thin straggle of smoke. He pointed.

'There they are. With a horse and a wagon, you'd think it was a gipsy camp.' Withers stopped, and nodded.

'I shall have to exercise great care in these negotiations, Derby. The last thing I wish to do is to arouse feelings of

131

antagonism. My attitude will be that we are all shipwrecked mariners with – ah – a common interest.'

Derby thought: I'm afraid that's going to be the trouble, that common interest. Once they know she's here. He saw that two of the Germans were standing up, watching them, so he held the flag up as high as he could and waved it about. Withers muttered grimly:

'We will advance now, Derby. Slowly and steadily. Please try to look friendly.'

'To you, or the Germans?'

'Don't be silly, Derby. Our very lives depend on this.'

They walked slowly up the slope, and now a group of four Germans detached themselves from the rest and moved down to meet them. The one in front was young, yellow-headed, about Derby's height and weight: there was a slight swagger in his walk.

When the two groups were about five yards apart, they halted, and Withers stepped forward to meet the German.

'Good-morning. I am Lieutenant-Commander Charles Witheringham, of the Royal Navy. Whom have I the honour of addressing?'

The large young man bowed slightly. There was something slightly contemptuous in his smile.

'Leutnant Otto Kreisch. Heil Hitler!' Withers said:

'How do you do. This —' he turned to Derby, 'this is Lieutenant-Commander Derby, also of the Royal Navy.'

'So. The fortunate gentleman who is playing beach games at night, no?' He saw Derby's look of astonishment, and chuckled. 'So. But, Herr Commander, why are you not bringing with you the so charming lady? We are all so wishing to – pay our respects to this fräulein. Nicht?' Behind him, the group of sailors laughed, and one of them shouted something in German that made Kreisch grin broadly. Derby felt his blood pressure rising, and he thought: Good job Withers is handling his: I'd have socked the swine by now. Withers told the German:

'I would like to speak to you, in private. Can you spare a few moments?'

132

Kreisch bowed. Withers turned back to Derby, and handed him the Mauser. He made sure that Kreisch saw it. Then they walked down on to the beach and sat side by side like two old friends on a fallen palm trunk. Derby waited, holding the pistol in his hand, and keeping his eyes on Withers.

They talked for about five minutes, and now and then one of them would wave a hand towards some part of the island. Once Withers turned and pointed at Derby, and Derby thought: He's telling him about the penalty for attempted rape.

Presently Withers and Kreisch got up off their log. Derby thought: It all looks very friendly. After Kreisch's opening remarks, it seemed impossible. Perhaps Withers should have been a diplomat, he thought: it would account for his being such a rotten sailor. They were coming back towards him, then they stopped, talking, and Kreisch bellowed some order to his camp. A voice called: 'Jawohl, Herr Leutnant!' and a man came running down the hill carrying a large, burning branch. He gave it to Withers. Derby heard Withers's voice:

'It's really *very* decent of you, Kreisch. When we're picked up, I shall make an official report on your co-operative spirit.'

Kreisch laughed. 'I do not think the Japanese will have so great interests in this, Herr Commander.'

Withers snapped: 'We expect a Bristish destroyer at any moment, Kreisch. I think you can rely on that.'

'For you, I am hoping so. We will be seeing, nicht?'

'As you say. I – I'm very pleased that we've had this little chat, Kreisch. And – er – thank you very much for *this*.' He indicated the smouldering branch: its heat was scorching his face.

'A pleasure, Herr Commander.' He bowed. 'Auf Wiedersehen.'

'Auf – er – good-bye, Kreisch. Good-bye.'

Withers came trotting up to Derby. He was smiling all over his face, and quite obviously he was very pleased with himself.

'Derby, a *resounding* success! Kreisch is *extremely* co-operative: why, he's even given us this – we can make a fire now, and cook fish!'

'How'd they get the fire going in the first place?'

'I didn't inquire, Derby.'

'Pity. Would have been interesting.... Well, what's the agreement, old man?'

'Wait till we get back to the others, Derby. I'll tell you all together. I'm delighted, Derby, delighted!'

Derby thought: It's fishy: there's a snag somewhere. He remembered Kreisch's expression and he thought: Old Withers has been had, I'm sure of it.

But when Withers had told them the details of the agreement, back at the camp, he couldn't see anything wrong. If the other side stuck to it, it was bound to work. He told Withers:

'Congratulations, old man. Well done!' Mary Lou nodded.

'It *is* good, isn't it. You can put away your pistol now, can't you?' Withers started.

'That reminds me, Derby. Please —' Derby handed it over. He and Spatter were piling odd scraps of wood and dry grass round the burning branch: in fact, it had begun to burn too fast, and now they were looking for green wood to slow it down. Spatter was the only one who hadn't so far commented on the agreement. Now he straightened up from the smoky glow of flame, and asked, pointing north:

'Commander. Ya gave the Krauts *that* half, huh?'

'Yes, indeed. That north hill, in fact all the island north of the low sand strip, and the beach on the west coast. We get this southern half and the east beach.'

'Uh-huh...' Spatter pointed again. 'And that sand strip is No-Man's-Land and neither side crosses it, that what ya said, Commander?'

'That is correct, Spatter.' Withers still looked smug. 'Do you approve of the plan?'

Spatter made a small hole in the sand with his toe, spat into it with remarkable accuracy, and smoothed the sand over.

'Commander, I'll tell y'a thing 'bout that goddam plan.'

'Yes, Spatter?'

'It goddam stinks. That's what. D'ya know why?' Withers simply stared at him, without answering. Spatter told him:

'We'll be thirsty, Commander. That's what. Only goddam stream is over on that hill there, the one you gave the Krauts.

There ain't a drop in your – our territory. Not one drop, so help me!' Withers stammered:

'You can't be sure of that, Spatter! You were only here a few hours before we arrived, you can't have —'

'We'd better take a look.' Derby interrupted because he felt sorry for Withers in his obvious panic. A minute ago. he'd been like a dog with two tails: now he was squirming under his mistake. Derby said: 'Mary Lou, let's go exploring. Coming?'

'With you, honey, *anywhere*!' He frowned at her.

'We'll start at the top of the hill and work down in a spiral.' Spatter shrugged, and told him, wearily:

'Count me out, Commander. I did it, yesterday. You'll be wasting your time.' Withers said, anxiously:

'I'd be grateful of you *would* check up thoroughly, Derby. Spatter may have overlooked some – some small spring. If the worst comes to the worst, I'll approach Kreisch again, and explain the situation. We'll make other arrangements, that's all.' Spatter snorted rudely.

'Think that basstud don't know what a hole he put us in?' Withers glared angrily at him.

'He's a most *co-operative* fellow!'

'Co-operative, hell! Th' way that Kraut knocked me down, sure, that's some co-operation, *I'd* say so!' Derby took Mary Lou's arm.

'Come on.' They set off uphill, and the voices, Spatter's snarling and Withers's querulous, faded behind them as the trees thickened and the ground grew steeper. Derby told her:

'I'm afraid Spatter's right. I thought Kreisch was a bit too friendly ... By the way: he knows about *us*.'

'What d'you mean, Bill – *us*?'

'Last night. They must have had one of them watching us. When Withers introduced me to the swine, he smirked and said: "Oh, you're the bloke that plays on the beach at night."'

'Hell. Did Withers catch on?'

'Of course not. But I'm afraid it'll have given the Huns ideas about you. That's the worry.'

She laughed. 'Didn't the little man threaten that he'd shoot anyone who besmirched my escutcheon?'

'I think he did. In fact I think he worries more about your welfare than anything else. But all the same, I don't like it a bit. That fellow Kreisch is a – well.'

'A what?'

'I don't know any word for it that I could use to you.' They didn't talk any more until they reached the top of the hill: it was a steep climb, the last bit, and they needed their breath.

Two hours later, when the sun was so accurately poised overhead that they cast no shadows as they stumbled hot and tired out of the trees into the open, they found Withers and Spatter roasting fish on sticks over the fire. The smell of it, and Withers, came to meet them.

'Well, Derby? Did you find water?'

Derby shook his head. 'Spatter's right, old man. I'm afraid there isn't any. We'll have to see Kreisch again.' He sniffed at the burning fish. How'd you catch them?'

Wither's face fell. 'Are you certain, Derby? None at all? Surely —'

'Not a drop. And no fruit either. I'm sorry.' He asked again: 'What were you using for bait, old man?'

'Eh? Oh, bait. A small piece of biscuit first, to catch a little one, then pieces of that to get the others. Derby – I think we'll have lunch before we go and find Kreisch.'

'Definitely. I'm famished.' He thought: It isn't going to be so good, seeing Kreisch again. Last time we met him on more or less equal terms: this time, we're beggars.

Mary Lou propped herself against a palm tree: its fronds, way up, threw a patch of shade about a foot wide around the base of the trunk. She spoke with her eyes closed against the heat.

'Let's have a drink, before we eat. I'm dying of thirst, after that hike.'

'I don't think we should.' Withers sounded apologetic, but firm. 'We've only this one cask left, and if Kreisch is really difficult —'

Spatter growled: 'You c'n bet on that, too.' Withers ignored him.

'If Kreisch is unco-operative, we shall have to make it last until we're rescued.'

Derby tried to brighten things up a bit. 'It might rain, old man. After all, it *did*. Then we could fill the casks by the balers.'

Mary Lou told them, tensely: 'If I don't have a drink soon I'll go mad! I'm parched, my throat hurts, I —'

'Steady, steady! Withers, old man, there must be a little left in the first cask, isn't there? We could share that out.' Withers looked round at them.

'Does everybody agree with that suggestion?' They all nodded, and Spatter said:

'Ladies first, I guess.' He was laying the smoking fish out in rows on a heap of leaves. 'I never seen fish this colour before, Commander. Sure hope they ain't poisonous.'

Derby carried the barrico over to Mary Lou, and worked the bung out. 'Here you are. One swig.' She lifted it to her mouth, and tilted her head back. Almost at once she lowered it, and stammered:

'I – I just – wet my lips – and it's – it's empty.' She told Derby: 'I hardly had any, it must've been —' She was looking up at him as if she expected him to think it was her fault that the thing was empty. He took it out of her hands.

'Don't worry. We can do without it.' Spatter said:

'Sure we can. C'mon, let's eat!'

X

'Derby – what on earth are they doing?'

The Germans were at work all along the northern edge of the sand strip that was now, through the Withers Agreement, a No-Man's-Land. On the slope that edged it on the German side, they were stacking wood and dead vegetation in heaps spaced out at regular intervals along the whole length of the border. There were eight or nine heaps, all told. Derby whistled.

'Spatter's right, old man. Kreisch knew what he was doing all right. Now he's making sure of it.'

'What d'you mean, Derby? I really don't —'

'He's building fires all along the line there. When they're burning, at night, it'll only take one sentry to guard the whole strip and spot anyone who tries to cross.'

'But why should anyone want to cross?'

'For water, old man. I'd already planned on it, myself, to nip up there in the dark. You see? Kreisch knows damn well we need water, and he's going to stop us getting it.'

'Oh, rubbish, Derby. He wouldn't be such a —'

'Have you forgotten he's a German?'

'Of course I haven't, Derby. But —'

'Well, we'll soon see. There he is.' Kreisch was standing alone, on the ridge, watching his men as they built the fires. He was just about opposite them.

'Hold your flag up, Derby. That's it. I'll attract his attention. . . .' Withers cupped his hands to his mouth, and shouted in his high, thin voice: 'I say, Kreisch!'

The German raised his head, and saw them. He stood there, with his hands on his hips, staring at them over a distance of fifty yards. Withers shouted again:

'Kreisch! I want to talk to you!' Kreisch called some remark to his men, and a murmur of laughter floated across the valley. He laughed, himself, then began to walk downhill, towards the border.

'Come, Derby.' They went down into No-Man's-Land, and within a few minutes they were face to face with the young German.

'The Herr Commander wishes to converse?'

'Indeed. Indeed I do, Kreisch. You see, that arrangement we came to this morning, while in all good faith I —'

'If the Herr Commander would speak a little slowly, please?'

'I beg your pardon. Kreisch: we have no water.'

'So?'

'So. I mean, no. None at all. The stream is on your side, and you must allow us to cross over every day at a fixed time to replenish our water casks. You will, won't you?'

'Please?'

Withers coughed. He said: 'Kreisch.' He pointed south, past Derby who was standing close behind him. 'Here, is no water.' He pointed now over Kreisch's shoulder. 'There, is water. . . . You understand?'

The young man inclined his head. 'The Herr Commander is most explicit.'

Withers stared at him for a moment without speaking. Then he resumed his explanation.

'We' – he pointed at himself and at Derby – 'we go *there*' – he pointed up the German hill – 'every day, get water. Yes?'

'No.' Kreisch smiled as he shook his head.

'But, Kreisch, we *must* have water!'

'Perhaps it will rain.' The German grinned offensively, and swung away. Derby told himself: I'd like to clobber that bloke. Perhaps I will, one day. Kreisch paused, and turned back to Withers.

'Herr Commander. If the lady come, I give her so much water she like.' Withers stood on his toes, and yelled:

'Certainly *not*! Spatter was right – you *are* a swine!'

'Captain Spatter, the American? I know him ... Herr Commander. If you come, or this – this friend of the lady, or the Herr Captain Spatter – my men will kill you. If the lady come – I give water.'

He turned away again, and began to climb the hillside. Derby thought: One day, come hell or high water, I'll hammer that character to a pulp: As Spatter would say: So help me.

I asked Derby: 'Did you ever make good that promise?'

We were in the Wheatsheaf, the local pub. It was only a hundred yards from the Derbys' farmhouse, quite close to the station where he'd met me the day before. Last night his story had taken so long in its telling that at about one in the morning his wife had insisted we should all go to bed. 'You can hear the rest of it in the morning,' she'd told me, and we'd trailed upstairs behind her like good little boys. Then this morning – the christening was to be at three in the afternoon – we'd come along to the Wheatsheaf, just he and I, for a pint or two of beer: the pint or two had become three or four and still Derby hadn't finished his yarn.

Now he twisted his glass round in the ring it had made on the table-top, and answered my question.

'Yes, I did. About a week after that interview with Kreisch, we were picked up by one of the Yank destroyers from Subic, and while the others were dancing about on the beach watching the destroyer's boat pull in, I got Kreisch to myself up in the trees. I beat the daylights out of him.'

I was awfully pleased to hear that. 'Good for you, Bill ... Time for one for the road, d'you think?' He glanced at his watch.

'Well, just one. Yes. It'll only take that long to tell you the rest.' I carried the empty glasses to the counter, and brought them back full.

'I suppose that second cask just about lasted the week, eh? Till you were picked up, I mean.'

Derby shook his head. 'Oh no, Mike. There's a lot more to it than that. Cheers, old man.'

'Cheers.'

Derby drank an inch off the top of his beer, and told me:
'It was Mary Lou who saved our lives.'

When they got back to the camp, they found Mary Lou
curled up and fast asleep. Spatter was sitting up against the
wall of the encampment, and he watched them as they came
trudging over the rise. He saw the expressions on their faces,
and nodded.

'Guess I was right, huh? We don't get no water outa Kraut
territory, I guess?'

'You were right, Spatter.' Derby flopped down on the sand.
'Dead right.'

'Uh-huh. What's his angle, Commander?'

'Angle?' Withers asked. 'What do you mean?'

'His line. What'd the guy say?'

'He refuses blankly to allow us to take any water, Spatter.
He said that if we tried to get any, he'd tell his men to kill us.
I'm afraid we're up against a brick wall.'

'It sure ain't no surprise to *this* boy.'

Derby murmured: 'Kreisch did make one suggestion.'

'An impossible one, Derby! I see no point at all in its being
discussed here.' Derby shrugged his shoulders.

'As you wish.' But Spatter was interested.

'Guess I'd kinda like to hear it, Commander.'

Withers shook his head. 'It's of no interest at all.'

'To me it is that, Commander. Seems to me I'm directly
concerned, I gotta right to be acquainted with it.'

'Very well.' Withers glanced at Mary Lou, to make sure she
was still sleeping. 'Kreisch said, Spatter, that if Mary Lou
went for the water, he would let her bring it back to us.' He
paused. 'Now that I've told you, we needn't mention the subject again, eh?'

Spatter nodded. 'I'm with you there, Commander. Nice
reasonable guy that, huh?' He chuckled to himself. 'Commander, how 'bout we have a small piece o' water, now?'

'At sundown, Spatter, I think. Do you agree, Derby? I'd

suggest sundown, and first thing in the morning, one mouthful each.'

'All right. But we're going to be pretty thirsty most of the time, at any rate.'

'I'm goddam thirsty right now!'

Withers said: 'We must endeavour to accustom ourselves to it, gentlemen. There is nothing else we can do. Unless Kreisch relents —'

'Not *that* sonofabitch!'

Withers coughed. 'I think I remember reading somewhere that in bathing, even in salt water, one absorbs a certain amount of moisture through the pores of the skin. We had better spend as much time as we can in the sea. I think in the shallows it should be safe from sharks, don't you, Derby?'

'Should be.'

Spatter nodded. 'Sure. We'll sit there all day in a row, like four gaddam ducks. That'll give Kreisch a laugh, all right.'

Derby suggested: 'Best conserve our energy. Move an talk as little as possible. Eh?'

'I agree with you, Derby. Absolutely. But I think I shall go and sit in the sea, now, until sundown.'

'I'll join that party, Commander.'

Derby said: 'I'm going to sleep.'

When he woke, the sun was almost setting: the palms cast long shadows down across the sand slopes, and already the air was cooler. But his tongue felt like sandpaper and there was a hard dry pain in his throat. He realized that he'd never been thirsty before, never in his life. He'd thought he had, but he hadn't. He turned his head, and found Mary Lou looking at him.

'About time too. You've been asleep *hours*, Bill.' Her voice was weak and edgy. 'Are you as thirsty as I am?'

'I could do with a drink.'

'I'd like a John Collins, with masses of ice. No – a Pimms, I think. In a bucket so I could put my whole head in and let it run out of my ears.'

'I'd settle for a pint of cold beer.' He stood up, and stretched. 'At least it's a bit cooler. Where are the others? Did they tell you about —'

'Yes. . . . They're down on the beach. Spatter's collecting driftwood for the fire, and Withers is after fish. For supper.' She told him: 'We're going to have a drink of water before we eat!'

He smiled. 'A few days ago, you and I were putting down gins one after the other just because there wasn't anything else to do. Now you're practically wild with excitement at the prospect of an ounce of warm water. . . . Here they come.'

'Ah, Derby! Awake at last. Look at this chap!'

'H'm. Quite a big one. Are you going to cook it before we have our drink, or after?' Withers hesitated.

'I think before. Otherwise we'll be thirsty again before we eat. Don't you think so?'

'Pity we couldn't have one drink before we eat, and another afterwards. That fish'll be pretty salty, I should imagine.'

'Yes. Yes, I know, Derby. But I don't see that it's possible, under the circumstances.' He took Derby's knife and cleaned the fish and filleted it. Then they each speared a fillet on a stick and roasted their own suppers.

Derby said: 'I'm going to eat before I have my water ration. I think I can get this down dry, all right.' Mary Lou nodded.

'Me too. Let's all eat first.' The others agreed. When they'd swallowed the fish, they sat and looked at the barrico. A minute passed, then Withers rose to his feet and walked over to it, and they all watched him.

'Derby, have you got your knife handy?'

'You used it to open the fish with.'

'So I did. So I did. Now where did I – ah!' He picked it up, and began to wipe the blade clean on a palm leaf. Mary Lou couldn't stand his slowness: she snapped:

'*Do* hurry up!' He glanced at her sharply.

'All in good time.' He snapped the blade in, and pulled out the spike. Then he bent over the cask and levered the bung out. 'There!' He straightened up. 'Spatter, will you pass me that baler? Just beside you. Wipe the sand out first, if you would.'

Spatter cleaned the tin out with his hand, and brought it over to Withers, who set it down carefully on level sand. He lifted the cask, and tilted it very slightly over the tin. He waited a moment, then, still very carefully, tilted it a bit more.

Frowning, he turned the cask still farther round. Farther and farther. His hands were shaking and sweat was running down his face. Presently he was holding the cask with its bung downwards over the empty tin, and nothing was coming out.

Withers put the cask down on the sand and turned to face the others. He could see by their faces that he didn't have to tell them it was empty. For a long time there was complete silence: then Mary Lou began to cry.

The dark came down slowly on slow-moving time. They'd all told her: We'll get you water, by morning you'll have something to drink, please don't worry! They were all of them far more thirsty than any of them had ever thought a man could get, but somehow it was for Mary Lou they said: We'll have water here by morning. The cool of the night was unreal, untrue, unlasting, in so few hours they'd be back in that oven. Each of them hated it for himself, but spoke of it for Mary Lou. Out of the three of them, Derby felt it more strongly than the others: strongly enough to work the thing out on logic and chances. The others wanted to go down to the dip again, to threaten Kreisch or plead with him: Derby, knowing that any such exertion would be nothing but a waste of strength, tried to argue them out of it.

'Wither – Spatter.' It was like talking through a fog. Through a blanket. Never been dying of thirst before, and seen no hope of water.

'Listen. Please, listen!' Still talk of seeing Kreisch, asking him, pleading with him. All of that's stupid. A waste of breath! Kreisch is the sort of German that makes Germans hated, and this is the ground that plant thrives in. Plead? If he gives way to pleading, the pleading's at an end. Kreisch is –

144

Kreisch. He was born that.

'Oh, listen!' Force? Kreisch lives by force. He respects only force. The muscle and the whip. He's only a man to himself when he controls the violence. The man who controls the source of the violence is his god. And he has nearly a dozen men there, including himself, against three of us. We'll – get ourselves killed, leave Mary Lou alone?

If you are pitted against an animal, do you have to get down on all fours?

She's talking in her sleep. It sounds like delirium. Like madness. Listen! D'you want to leave her alone, like this? Better not listen, she isn't saying anything. She isn't saying anything you'd understand. She's asleep and twisting about on the sand and talking to herself: it'd be best not to listen. She isn't talking sense. My name? Any name, she's delirious. Yours later, if you listened. Better not to listen.

Listen to me instead. Withers – Spatter – I think I've got it! Really, I think with any luck at all this ought to work! Withers —

They're asleep, both of them. Talking one minute, asleep the next. Perhaps they've been asleep longer than I know: perhaps I just heard their voices and they weren't talking.

Funny. I never really imagined thirst. Not real thirst. It's enough to —

There was a plan, wasn't there? Wasn't I trying to tell them about it? Had it all in my mind, sure of it, I was going to tell them that – that —

Swim. Yes, that was it. Swim. And tow the barrico on a length of twine astern of me and – the twine's in that boat's bag —

Of course. They've fires along the strip so I couldn't cross there, they'd see me. I'll swim out and round, towing the cask, and land behind where they are and get to the water. Fill it and get back here the same way before dawn.

Better start. If I don't, none of us'll see another moon like that one.

145

He found the reel of twine in the boat's bag and cut about twenty feet off it: enough to have it doubled and tow the cask clear astern of him as he swam. He lashed one doubled end of it around the cask and the other to a separate string around his waist. He had the knife on that other loop, too. Movement and action seemed to have cleared his mind: he felt as if he'd come out from under an anaesthetic. With the twine trailing behind him he picked the cask up and carried it down through the trees to the beach, and waded slowly into the sea.

The tide was out, and the moon rode high in the clear black sky. The rocks, up at the other end of the beach, stood high out of the still water: the sea was dead flat, yet at the rocks' point, where the boat had almost struck, he could see even from this distance a flicker of white where they cut the sea's slightest movement. To Derby, that flash of white was a warning that he'd have to swim with infinite caution: any splash or disturbance of the surface would show up a mile away, and then they'd be waiting for him to land.

He waded very slowly out into the deepening water. The shelf was gradual, and he was fifteen yards out from the beach by the time the water reached even to his waist. He got down in it, up to his neck, then started to swim with his arms and push with his feet on the sandy bottom: the cask towed easily, lightly, astern of him. When he was almost out if his depth, he swung north, towards the point of the rocks. As he swam, he kept his eyes on the beach and on the shoulder of the northern hill. The beach was white under the moon, striped with the shadows of palms. He thought: This isn't much better than doing it in daylight. The moon was so bright that the Germans hadn't bothered to light their watch fires: nobody could have crossed that white strip of No-Man's-Land and not be seen. He thought: Kreisch has the date on his side, too. The bastard. He looked ahead at the rocks: another twenty yards, no more. He thought: I'm a bloody fool, to have started this now: should have waited for the moon to go down. But he knew, too, that if he'd waited he might have fallen into a coma, and never started at all.

Close to the rocks, he stopped swimming and let the drift of the tide draw him into their shadow. The cask still floated out in the moonlight, a dark blot on the silver surface, so he hauled it close in beside him out of the moon's reach. He rested, his knees on the smooth underwater rock that the boat had hit with her keel, and searched the beach for sentries.

He couldn't see any. Where the rock spur climbed into the island, there was a dark edge of shadow, and he thought: This isn't going to be so difficult, after all! As long as they haven't already spotted me, I've got a chance. The tricky bit was going to be the dozen yards from the shadow at the water's edge to the shelter of the trees. Everything depended on luck: there could be a German sentry right there in the trees, where he'd be invisible. Derby thought: But there's no reason why there should be, unless Kreisch is brighter than he looks: unless he's Combined-operations-minded. In any case, there's no way of avoiding the risk: I simply have to hope for the best.

Holding the cask close in behind him, he began to slip inshore, keeping well into the rocks' shadow. Nothing moved on the beach. He moved very carefully, terrified that he might stumble on some jutting piece of rock and make a splashing that would attract the enemy's attention. When the water shallowed, he crawled through it on his hands and knees, keeping his body under water as long as there was enough to cover it. At the sea's edge he stopped again, crouching down against the side of the tall rock: keeping his eyes on the beach and the slopes that led up from it, and working with slow and painful caution, he cut the twine at his waist, and at the cask. In case he might need it later, he rolled it up and stuffed it into his pocket.

There was no movement that he could see, and the only sound was the faint whisper of the sea along the beach. He took the cask under his left arm and crawled out of the water. At once he felt nakedly exposed: there was no knowing how effective this strip of shadow would be, seen by some watcher up there on the hillside. Well – this was the moment. No good crouching here waiting for it! Gripping the cask tightly under his arm, he rose to his feet.

Ahead of him, the beach was clear and empty. Brilliantly

white: a searchlight wouldn't have made it any brighter. Derby moved out of the shadow, and began to walk straight up towards the trees. He'd thought of running, but had decided that if he was going to be seen he'd be seen either way, and walking made less noise. He watched the trees ahead, and kept glancing down too, at the sand ahead, to make sure there was nothing that might trip him. He was only a couple of yards from that dark line of trees, and he was thinking: I've done it, I'm *there*! He took one more pace forward towards the trees. and a German sailor stepped out into the moonlight. Two others joined the first. They carried heavy sticks, like clubs, and for a clear moment they stood together in a line, looking at him and not saying a word.

Derby, too, stood still, for that shocked second. Then, without conscious thought, he twisted and ran to his left, along the line of the trees. A heavy swipe from one of the sticks glanced off his right shoulder as he turned. The Germans shouted, and he thought: I've had it, there'll be others ahead now, to cut me off. He thought: Well, I'll give the swine something to think about, before I'm finished. He was running harder than he'd ever run in his life and he stumbled, some root caught his foot: he staggered off-balance down the slope of the beach, struggling wildly for a foothold: he'd almost steadied himself when he saw the first German coming: he dropped down on to one knee, and as the fellow flung himself forward Derby straightened and jerked the cask up hard into his face. The man staggered back, screaming and clasping his face in his hands, and Derby used the cask again, crashing it down on the second man as he came in in a sort of clumsy rugger tackle. The German reeled back, aiming a shot at Derby with his stick: it caught him across the left side of his face and it hurt like hell. If the fellow'd been squarely on his feet when he'd delivered the blow. it'd have been the end. Derby roared in pain and anger, and jumping inside the arc of the stick as it swung again he brought his knee hard up into the man's groin and at the same time smashed the cask into his face. Derby glanced round: the third German hadn't appeared at all, and the first one, the one who'd probably had his nose broken, was cantering away into the trees still holding his face and shouting at the top of his voice. The one Derby'd dealt with last was on his hands and knees, spitting blood and teeth and holding his groin and groaning. Derby kicked him hard on the temple with his heel, to keep him quiet, then ran as hard as he could straight along the moonlit beach. Up to his right he could still hear shouts from the man who'd run away, and from a greater distance German voices were answering. They sounded excited, and surprised.

The beach was clear, all along its length. Derby was grateful to the man who was doing the shouting, because he'd be attracting any potential reinforcements in his own direction, instead of down this way to cut him off. He ran on, his heart pounding and his breath short and his head singing from that vicious stick. He passed the eastern end of the strip called No-Man's-Land, and, realizing that he was now in the comparative safety of British territory, he slowed to a walk.

There was no shouting, now, from behind, but as he turned and glanced back he saw a sudden tongue of flame shoot up, and then another farther along, and he thought: they're lighting the fires. I've made them windy, put them on their toes: we haven't a chance of getting over there again. He thought miserably: I've done a damn sight more harm than good.

Slowly he climbed the slope from the beach to the camp. The side of his face smarted and ached, where the German's stick had hit him, and the sheer impossibility of passing another day without water screamed a much deeper pain into his mind. In desperation he thought: I'll have another go. There's nothing else for it. I'll wait till the moon's down, then I'll cross over the island and swim up the other coast and land above their camp. They won't expect me there, right on their doorstep: they'll be watching the sand strip, and the other beach.

He told himself: I'd better not get caught. I won't be as popular as I have been up to now. But I'll try it: wait till the moon's down, get a few hours' sleep, and try then.

He staggered up into the camp. His whole body ached, it cried out for rest and more than that for water. The fire still burned, and close to its glowing circle sprawled Withers and

Spatter. Derby dropped the cask on to the sand, and they didn't wake. He looked round, and wondered: Where's Mary Lou? But he was too tired and too sore to worry. He thought: She can't be far away. Probably under those trees, up there, in their shade, out of the moonlight. This is much tougher for her than it is for us. Poor little —

He curled up with his face turned away from the moon, and fell asleep.

'Derby! Derby! My *dear* fellow!'

Derby rolled over on his back, and opened his eyes. It was daylight. With a sense of defeat, he thought: I've slept right through!

Withers was bending over him, grasping both his shoulders, shaking him and beaming into his face.

'Derby, I'll get you a medal for this! I'll get you a Victoria Cross! My *dear* fellow!'

Derby sat up, and pushed Withers away. Spatter took his place immediately. The American grabbed Derby's right hand and pumped it up and down.

'Commander. Shakin' your hand is an honour. An honour, sir. I'll see the United States expresses its appreciation, its gratitood, sir, in a sootable manner.'

Derby noticed that Spatter had tears in his eyes. He thought: They're all mad. Stark, raving mad. Blinking, he looked over their heads: Mary Lou was standing just behind them, making faces at him. She seemed to be trying to convey some private message. He thought: My God, they're all cracked! Mary Lou was pointing at one of the casks – not the one he'd taken with him, the other one – and she was trying to tell him something terribly important. He gave her the benefit of the doubt, and tried to understand, but he couldn't make anything of her expressions or gestures. He stared blankly at her, and shook his head in utter bewilderment.

Withers pushed Spatter aside, and grasped Derby's shoulder.

'Derby, you've saved our lives. Without that water we'd

have never —'

'Water?' He looked at Mary Lou again. An impossible idea was taking root in his mind. 'Water?'

She nodded violently, pointing at the cask beside her, then pointing at him. Her lips framed a word: he stared at her, and she did it again. He read the word: *Please!*

Spatter murmured, gently: 'The guy's kinda shocked, I guess. Must've been pretty rough, Commander: guess y' didn't just walk in an' take it, huh?' He touched Derby's cheek, where that stick had landed, and Derby flinched away at the sudden stab of pain. He was thinking: When I got back, she wasn't here. He tried to force his mind back, to get some picture into it of what he'd seen then, to remember whether or not that other cask had been there in the sand. But he couldn't get to it at all. He looked up at her again, wondering, and she put her two hands together under her chin as if she was saying her prayers, and again her lips shaped that word: *Please!*

Withers asked him, in a tone of deep respect: 'Derby. If it became necessary, could you do it again? I mean, would you be able to fill the other cask, the same way?'

'Could I —' He looked up over Withers's shoulder. Mary Lou was nodding violently. She wanted him to say yes. Derby closed his eyes, and leant back on his elbows on the sand. He told Withers, tiredly:

'I suppose so. I dare say I could.' He thought: It'd certainly explain why there aren't any Huns down on the beach to cut me off.

XI

'And there,' said Derby, 'you have it. Now we'd better move, or we'll be in the doghouse.' He poured the last of his beer down his throat: I'd already finished mine, and to tell the truth I was feeling rather full of beer.

'Bill.' I had to know the answer to this. 'Did she – I mean, when she went over for the water, did she —'

'Hush.' Derby raised a long forefinger in admonition. 'The question you are about to ask is one of extreme delicacy. Anyway, your guess is as good as mine.' He chuckled as he pushed the door open. 'Carry on, Mike. We'd better step on it.' We turned left, up the hill. Derby burped slightly, and told me:

'You know, I felt a bit spare, taking the kudos for her —'

'Diplomacy?' He laughed.

'I suppose you could call it that.'

'Did she – you – ever repeat the operation?'

'No. But we were going to. Water was getting low, and the others expected me to do something about it. Mary Lou told me she'd fix it – I was to cover up for her, You see, Mike, by this time I couldn't very well get out of it. I was to disappear for four or five hours, then meet her at the border and take the water from her. She'd slope into camp from the other direction, and if anyone'd missed her she'd say she'd been up to the top of the hill to watch my movements on the other side. She had all the answers, that girl. Fortunately, the destroyer turned up that afternoon.'

'But, Bill, *four of five hours* —'

'I know, old man. I know. But we mustn't jump to unkind conclusions, eh?' We walked on up the muddy road in silence. Then I asked him:

'What's happened to the others, now? Withers on the beach, I suppose?'

Derby nodded. 'Yes, he's retired. But – you'll find this hard to believe, old man – he's an Admiral!'

'Don't be a clot, Bill!' I thought: He's had too much beer.

'It's true, Mike. He's an Admiral. He's coming to lunch – you'll see him presently. He's going to be the other godfather: make a good one, I dare say. Very conscientious bloke, old Withers.' He chuckled to himself again as we turned into the farm entrance. The mud here was about a foot deep.

I shook my head. 'I can't see it, Bill. *Withers? An Admiral?*' I'd seen some pretty odd things during my time in the Navy, but this just wasn't possible. Derby put his hand on my shoulder as we sloshed down the lane.

'S'fact, old man. He got a terrific recommend, after we were picked up. Power of Command, maintaining iron control of prisoners under extraordinary conditions, keeping up our morale – all that sort of thing. Frankly, I wasn't too keen on taking a lot of glory for myself out of Mary Lou's nocturnal adventures, so I let him take it all, and of course he did. Well, he didn't *know*, damn it! They gave him a brass hat and sent him to some semi-diplomatic job in Germany, and in no time at all the little man's hands were just about touching the ground under the weight of four stripes. Then his area suddenly increased in importance, or something, and bang – he was a Commodore! I ask you!'

I certainly found it about as much as I could believe.

'And you say he's an Admiral, now?'

'Ah. Admiral Sir Charles Witheringham. After Germany, they promoted him and stuck him in the Admiralty. He did pretty well, there, signing letters or something. Then he signed one he shouldn't have signed, and it caused a mutiny in the West Indies. It was all hushed up – if it'd come out, the Government might have come unstuck. So they gave Withers a knighthood and plonked him on the beach. He lives near here.'

We rounded the cowshed, and headed for the back door. Those yellow dogs of Derby's were standing there, up to their hocks in slush, baying unhappily at a small black kitten on top of the barn door. Derby told me:

'They're awfully stupid, those dogs. Eat too much, too. . . .

In you go; wipe your boots inside, old man, it's too dirty out here. I'm afraid we're late, we'd better go straight in.'

'Can I wash first?'

'Don't worry about that, old man.' He pushed open the sitting-room door, and dragged me in. Withers was standing with his behind right up against the fire: he was wearing a double-breasted navy-blue suit, and he looked like a seedy little Merchant Navy steward lost in a big city. Derby greeted him.

'Ah, Withers! Sorry, old man – we were delayed. Unavoidably of course. D'you remember Mike Fairley? Used to be my Number One, in *Slayer*. Mike – this is – er – Admiral Sir Charles Witheringham.' Withers peered at me.

'Fairley? Fairley. Yes, of course! *Fairley!* How are you, Fairley?'

I assured him that I was in the best of health. Derby asked him:

'Where're the girls, old man?'

'I think they're looking at your son, Derby. Extraordinary, the length of time women can spend simply staring at infants. Extraordinary. What?'

I nodded at him, cautiously. I couldn't think of anything else to do, really. Then I heard the door opening behind me, and Withers stepped forward, crowing.

'My dear! You have been a time! Er – Fairley – my dear, I wonder if you met this – er – officer? Fairley, d'you remember my wife, eh? Eh?'

I felt as if I'd had an electric shock. I goggled at her, and stammered: 'Yes! Oh yes! I – I *do*!' Lady Witheringham took my hands between her two soft, warm ones, and smiled into my eyes. I thought, vaguely: No wonder he got promoted! But I was tongue-tied, I could only stare at her in mixed astonishment and admiration.

Glancing to my left, I saw that Derby had turned his back: he was bending slightly forward with a handkerchief at his face and his shoulders were shaking. I realized that he'd kept this secret on purpose: he'd just wanted to see my face when I met her, and now he'd seen it the whole thing was more than he could stand.

I looked back at the incredibly attractive creature in front of me, and, at last, found my tongue.

'Lady Witheringham, I —'

'Oh, *Mike*! You *used* to call me Mary Lou!' Behind me, Withers coughed.

'Quite right. No point in formality – er – Fairley.' Mary Lou was still holding my hand and looking into my eyes. I murmured:

'Mary Lou!' I hadn't meant to say it, it just came out as if her glance had drawn it out of me.

She breathed: 'That's right, Mike!' and she squeezed my hand more firmly. Then Derby's wife shot into the room, almost at a run.

'Lunch, everybody! Come along, or we'll be late at the church, and the poor old vicar'll be livid. . . . Bill, where *have* you two been?'

I don't remember much about that lunch. It was a hurried affair, I know, and nobody talked much: Derby opened a bottle of wine, and on top of all that beer it made my head swim. The only other thing I can remember is that I found it physically impossible to take my eyes off Mary Lou.

Afterwards, we were left alone for a few minutes. She began by scolding me, gently, for having remained a bachelor all this time. Then she asked me:

'You're based at Portsmouth?'

'Yes. Dear old Blockhouse. I love the place.'

'And spend wild week-ends in London, I suppose?'

'Well —' I shrugged. She smiled, and said casually:

'There's a show I want to see *so* badly. The new Noël Coward. This is the last month of it, too, I'm afraid.' She put her hand on my arm, and told me: 'I've a little *pied-à-terre* in Town, but I can never persuade Charles to come up. The traffic worries him.' I thought: She might be talking about a dog, or a horse. She murmured: 'I suppose I shall have to see that play alone, if I see it at all.'

Some madness took possession of me. Well, perhaps the beer and the wine helped it along. I forgot I was talking to Lady Witheringham: I asked Mary Lou:

'Would you come with *me*? This next week-end?'

'Why, Mike! What a *lovely* idea! Only – look, Mike dear, don't say a word in front of Charles, will you? He's so – touchy, sometimes.' She ran across the room and delved in her handbag, then came back and gave me a card. 'That's the address and telephone. I'll be there soon after lunch on Saturday. Don't lose the card, will you, Mike?'

I shook my head. The suggestion was so silly that it didn't need an answer. I told her: 'I'll book the seats, and ring you on Saturday afternoon. Shall we have supper somewhere after the show? Dance?' I was thinking of a night-club. And I was talking fast, to get it fixed before we were interrupted. She squeezed my arm.

'That *would* be fun, Mike. We'll start with drinks in my flat, shall we? It's only a tiny little mews place, but —'

She moved away, slightly, and turned so that she was facing the window. She finished: 'And in the summer, the roses are really *too* beautiful!'

Withers beamed at us from the doorway. He beckoned.

'Come along, my dear. Come on, Fairley. We're all ready, now.' Mary Lou moved sweetly across the room, and took his arm. Just as they passed out through the door that led to the yard, she glanced back at me over her shoulder, and winked.

THOSE ABOUT TO DIE   30p
Daniel P. Mannix

"He started forward toward the melee, blood from his wounded side filling up the footprints made by his right foot as he staggered on. The armed *venator* and the spearman exchanged looks. The crowd was shouting, 'No Carpophorus, no!' But Carpophorus paid no attention to them. He was going to get another tiger or die trying."

This infamous but completely factual book tells the story of the Roman Games, where two armies of 5,000 men fought to the death in a show lit at night by human torches. It was the costliest, cruellest spectacle of all time. And hundreds of thousands still crave to satisfy their curiosity about the sport every year – *Those About to Die* is a constantly reprinting bestseller. No other title gives the full facts and paints such a realistic scene: this is an all-the-way book about man's greatest aberration.

KING OIL 30p
Max Catto

The voice of my beloved! he cometh,
Leaping upon the mountains, skipping upon
    the hills.   SONG OF SOLOMON

Frank Dibbler, already a millionaire who
wants to be an oil king and become founder
of a dynasty that will perpetuate his name in
the future industrial America that he
foresees, chooses as his wife the daughter of a
Spanish grandee, taking her on the long
hazardous journey from the genteel pomp of
Seville to the vast, untamed ranch-land of
Texas.

This epic yarn is Max Catto's finest and most
gripping novel.

PROVIDENCE ISLAND   60p

Calder Willingham's bestselling powerhouse of a novel

The bold story of one man and two women shipwrecked on an uninhabited Caribbean island where all of modern civilisation's taboos are stripped away – and three lives are irrevocably changed.

The erotic power and uncompromising readability of *Providence Island* will shock some and delight many. Few will deny it as the work of a master storyteller and many will recognise its profound human warmth.

Calder Willingham is the controversial bestselling author of *Eternal Fire, End as a Man, Geraldine Bradshaw, A Natural Child, To Eat a Peach* and *The Gates of Hell* (all available in Mayflower).